PRAISE FOR

THE LIFE AND CRIMES OF
HOODIE ROSEN

"*The Life and Crimes of Hoodie Rosen* is a deeply authentic story about the terror and glory of encountering the outside world without sacrificing who you are—and who you want to be. It's touching, tragic, and as Jewish as your bubbe's cholent."

—GAVRIEL SAVIT,

NEW YORK TIMES BESTSELLING AUTHOR OF *ANNA AND THE SWALLOW MAN*

"Isaac Blum has the rare talent of telling searing, visceral truths in a witty, funny, punchy way that almost makes you forget that he's opened the window to share something personal, real, heartbreaking and hopeful. *The Life and Crimes of Hoodie Rosen* is a vital voice in Jewish YA canon."

—KATHERINE LOCKE,

SYDNEY TAYLOR HONOR AUTHOR OF *THE GIRL WITH THE RED BALLOON*

"Hoodie's irreverent and witty voice draws you in immediately; though the novel deals with heavy topics, the pace never lags. I came for the Jewish rep and stayed for Hoodie and Anna-Marie. Can't wait to see more from Isaac Blum!"

—LEAH SCHEIER,

SYDNEY TAYLOR HONOR AUTHOR OF *THE LAST WORDS WE SAID*

"*The Life and Crimes of Hoodie Rosen* is a wry and poignant coming-of-age tale about trying to reconcile two different worlds. As Hoodie begins to reckon with the way his Orthodox community fits into their new town—and the way he fits into his community—he must also ask questions about love, family, and friendship. Both humorous and heartrending, readers will devour this book."

—HANNAH REYNOLDS,

AUTHOR OF *THE SUMMER OF LOST LETTERS*

"Keenly observant and frequently hilarious, readers will root for Hoodie as he navigates first love, makes mistakes and ultimately trusts his heart."

—LAURA SIBSON,

AUTHOR OF *THE ART OF BREAKING THINGS* AND *EDIE IN BETWEEN*

THE LIFE AND CRIMES OF
HOODIE ROSEN

BY ISAAC BLUM

PHILOMEL BOOKS

PHILOMEL BOOKS
An imprint of Penguin Random House LLC, New York

First published in the United States of America by Philomel Books, an imprint of Penguin Random House LLC, 2022

Copyright © 2022 by Isaac Blum

Philomel Books is a registered trademark of Penguin Random House LLC.

Visit us online at penguinrandomhouse.com.

Library of Congress Cataloging-in-Publication Data is available.

Printed in the United States of America

ISBN 9780593525821

1st Printing

LSCH

Edited by Talia Benamy

Design by Lily K. Qian

Text set in Adobe Caslon Pro

For my parents

CHAPTER 1

in which I celebrate Tu B'Av by taking the first step toward my own ruination

LATER, I TRIED TO EXPLAIN to Rabbi Moritz why it was ironic that my horrible crime was the thing that saved the whole community. He didn't get it, either because he was too angry, or because his head was filled with other thoughts, or because the man has no sense of humor.

I don't think it's funny now—it ruined my life, put me in intensive care, and humiliated me and my family on a global scale. But I found it funny at the time.

It all started on Tu B'Av, which is one of the more obscure Jewish holidays. I'm Orthodox, but even I couldn't recall what the holiday was about. I only remembered when I looked out the window and saw the girl in white. She was on the sidewalk across the street.

I was in halacha class, learning about Jewish law. We were talking about ritual hand-washing. Rabbi Moritz paced back and forth in front of the whiteboard, reading from the *Shulchan Aruch*, making the occasional Hebrew or English note on the board.

I was a little distracted because Moshe Tzvi Gutman was slurping cereal next to me, and a little distracted because Ephraim Reznikov was reading his copy of the *Shulchan Aruch* out loud but out of sync with Rabbi Moritz. But I was mostly distracted trying to remember what the heck Tu B'Av was about.

I couldn't ask my buddy Moshe Tzvi because he would make fun of me for not knowing. Moshe Tzvi studies really hard, and he makes you feel like an ignorant schmuck if you aren't as learned as he is. So I just stared out the window as though the answer would be out on the street. And then it was.

Because now the girl was dancing, making various motions with her hands, swinging her body around in little circles.

Which made me remember that Tu B'Av had something to do with dancing girls and the grape harvest—the grape harvest was pretty big back in biblical times. During the grape harvest, all the unmarried girls of Jerusalem went out into the vineyards where the harvest was happening, and they danced, wearing only plain white robes. Because all these girls were wearing plain white robes, the boys didn't know if the girls were rich or poor, or even which tribe they were from. It created a level playing field, and the boys could choose a wife without thinking about if she was poor, or if she was from some undesirable rival tribe.

The girl outside wasn't wearing a white robe, because it was the twenty-first century. She wore a white T-shirt, its short sleeves revealing skinny arms. The shirt ended just above a pair of shorts that left most of her legs exposed. The legs ended at a pair of white Adidas sneakers, striped blue.

She was dancing. But why was she dancing? There was nobody on the sidewalk with her but a small white dog. I thought it was strange behavior, but maybe gentile girls danced for their dogs all the time. I had no idea. I wasn't supposed to look at gentile girls. I guess there were Jewish girls who dressed that way too, but certainly not any I knew. And if she was a Jewish girl dressed like that, I wasn't allowed to look at her either.

When she stopped dancing, she walked over to the base of a tree, bent down, and picked up a cell phone. Maybe she'd recorded her dance? She stood up, looked over, and made eye contact with me. Or, I thought she did. It was hard to tell from that distance, but when she looked up at me—or at the school—I reflexively looked away, up at the board, at Rabbi Moritz. The contrast between the girl and the rebbe couldn't have been starker. He wore a heavy black suit and had an enormous beard. And Moritz was spitting as he talked. He had a little bit of saliva on his upper lip.

"Why, according to the text," the rebbe asked, "must we wash our hands upon rising in the morning? Why, before we walk four cubits, must we wash?"

Reuven was all over it. "We have left the chance for evil spirits to come onto us in the night. So we wash them off, the spirits."

"Amazing. As Reuven said, we have left ourselves

vulnerable," Moritz went on, his voice rising to "vulnerable," pausing, then descending, "not only to the spirits of evil, but what else?" His voice rose again, and the question came out in a high-pitched squeak. "What else?"

Reuven again: "The spirits have come and, depending on how you read it, our souls have departed, right?"

"Correct. Our souls have departed through our hands. Through cleansing, and through the Modeh Ani prayer, our souls return and we are ready for service of HaShem." Everything Moritz said came back around to servicing God.

"What if you wear gloves?" asked Moshe Tzvi. He was still working on his cereal, but he paused to gesticulate with his plastic spoon, spraying little drops of milk across his desk. "You know, while you sleep. Must you still wash?"

Rabbi Moritz paused in his pacing. "This is a good question," he said. "I would say, based on the text, that the gloves would keep your soul in your body. Though of course this would be impractical, sleeping in gloves."

"Okay," Moshe Tzvi said, scratching his bare chin. "Now what if the gloves have a small hole in them? What are the dimensions of the soul? And how . . . squeezy is it?"

"I think the question is not how big the hole is in the gloves, but whether or not the wearer of the gloves is *aware* of the hole," said Rabbi Moritz.

This is always the question. Judaism has rules for just about everything, from how to slaughter your animals, how to watch television without violating Shabbos (our Sabbath, our day of rest), to when and for how long you have to refrain from eating on fast days (of which there are many). But the trick is that you only have to follow the rules if you know about them. If you're a Jew, but you don't *know* you're a Jew, you don't have to follow *any* of the rules. It's like if you went to Walmart and stole a bunch of things, and then the police came and they were about to arrest you, and you were like, "Wait, I didn't *know* it was illegal to take this stuff without paying," and the police were like, "Oh, okay, our apologies. Have a good day. Enjoy the free TV."

I had a question for the rebbe, but I was too busy staring out the window, and it slipped away. So too had the girl—she wasn't there anymore.

"What if the hole is pretty big?" Moshe Tzvi asked. "Big enough that you can't plausibly deny knowing about it? Maybe you turn your hand over so you can't see the hole, but you can feel that it's there."

"Then you have to wash."

Rabbi Moritz picked his book back up, and was about to turn the page, but Moshe Tzvi wasn't satisfied. "What if Hoodie is sleeping in his gloves, and he knows there's a hole in his glove, but then I bash him over the head with a very heavy piece of pipe, and he forgets about the hole in his glove due to his head trauma?"

Rabbi Moritz considered, nodding his head a few times in a slow rhythm. "It would depend on his state of mind upon awakening, after he's slept. Can we move on?"

"No," said Moshe Tzvi. "We haven't talked about sleeping in mittens."

"Oy, Moisheee."

Moritz did move on. Now he was talking about the hand-washing itself, how to do it right. I wasn't listening, partly because if I didn't know the right way, I could do it how I wanted. But mostly I wasn't listening because I was too distracted, staring out the window, looking for the Tu B'Av girl in white. Now that she'd disappeared I couldn't be sure that I'd seen her at all. She could have been just a figment of my imagination, a physical manifestation of my thoughts about Tu B'Av, what my mind thought a dancing tribeless grape-harvest girl would look like today.

I had to know for sure.

I got up from my desk. Moshe Tzvi handed me his Styrofoam cereal bowl as I walked by. I left the room, slurping the sweet leftover milk. I tossed the bowl in the can outside and put on my black hat.

When I took walks, I always liked to wear my suit jacket and hat. I wanted to look sharp and distinguished. "Respectable" was the word my dad always used.

It was still summer, and the neighborhood smelled like grass clippings. I could hear the buzz of a distant mower. A welcome breeze swayed the trees that lined the streets.

Usually I walked slowly, lost in my thoughts. I paid no attention to where I was, or where I was going. But today I moved with purpose, walking the grid of streets in a systematic fashion, making sure I at least glanced down every road.

I saw her on Cellan. She was pulling at the leash, trying to drag the dog along, but the little thing had found an interesting scent at the base of a tree, and he was digging in, keeping his weight low, trying to hold his ground.

I walked toward her slowly, growing more and more nervous with each step. I'd never spoken to one of the neighborhood girls. Yeshiva students aren't allowed to talk to girls, let alone girls dressed like this one. I didn't really *want* to talk to her. It was more like I *had* to. I was drawn toward her, as though pulled by some kind of sci-fi tractor beam.

It was Tu B'Av. She was dressed in white. Maybe this was what God wanted from me.

She was too busy struggling with the dog to see me approach. I tried to think of a clever way to start a conversation. "Um," I said. After weighing many outstanding options, I'd decided "Um" was the best choice.

"Oh," she said, and looked up.

The dog took the opportunity to scramble toward the tree, sniffing it audibly. While the girl stared at me, the dog peed on the tree.

The girl looked at me like I had eight heads.

"Nice hat," she said.

She had deep brown eyes, and jet-black hair pulled up in a scrunchie.

"Thanks," I said. "It's a Borsalino." The hat was my most prized possession, a bar mitzvah gift from my parents. When she didn't respond, I told her the hat was Italian.

"Okay," she said.

I shifted my weight uncomfortably. I was sweating. The

breeze had died and it was blazing hot out, so maybe that was it.

I wanted to get away. I could tell that she did too. When the dog started pulling on the leash, a look of relief appeared on her face, and she took a step away from me.

"What's the dog's name?" I asked. I hadn't meant to ask. I'd meant to say nothing. I'd meant to let her walk away so I could peacefully live out the rest of my life without ever feeling this uncomfortable again. But I'd spoken, almost against my will.

"Borneo," she said. "Like the island."

I'd never heard of Borneo, but I didn't want her to know that. "Oh yeah," I said, "the island. In the . . . ocean." That's where the islands were, right? In the ocean. "What's your name?" I asked before I could stop myself.

"Anna-Marie." And she gave a last name too, Diaz-something, but I missed it.

"Crap," I said. I basically didn't have any control over my words at this point.

"Huh?" she asked.

When I asked her name, I'd been holding out hope she'd be a Chaya or an Esther. But no. She was an Anna-Marie. Just Anna would have provided a sliver of hope. I knew from the shorts that she wasn't super observant, definitely not frum, like me. But unhyphenated Anna could have been a Jew at least, if a secular one. Some secular Jews lived in the area. There was a reform synagogue and a delicatessen in the next town.

But Anna-*Marie*? There literally wasn't a more goyishe name.

When Anna-Marie moved her arm to pull on the dog's

leash, a cross appeared above the collar of her shirt. It jumped back and forth on a silver chain just above her bare collarbone. I watched it in despair.

She moved to leave again.

"I'm Hoodie," I said.

"Hoodie?"

"Like the sweatshirt." I motioned as though to pull a hood over my head.

Anna-Marie reached out to shake hands. I looked at her hand. She had slender fingers, each nail carefully painted an aquamarine color. Aquamarine. Anna-Marie. I wanted to shake Anna-Marie's aquamarine hand desperately. I looked behind me to see if anybody was watching. Nobody was. But I still couldn't do it. I was a bar mitzvah, and I wasn't married to her, so I wasn't allowed to touch her. I just stared at her hand until she took it away.

"Okay, Hoodie. Borneo and I are gonna go."

"Do you live around here?" I asked.

"No. I took an Uber here to walk the dog."

I laughed, and some of the tension melted. "Stupid question," I said. "It was good to meet you, Anna-Marie."

She took a step away, then turned back. "Hey," she said, and she took out her phone. "What's your Insta? I'll follow you."

I knew she meant Instagram, a picture app people had on their smartphones. I wasn't allowed to use it, but I didn't want her to know that. I reached into my pocket and took out my phone. When she saw it, Anna-Marie broke into a huge smile. It lit up her whole face. Then she started laughing. "You have a *flip* phone?" she asked. "Wait, wait. Hold on. I have to snap this. Cassidy will *never* believe it."

I smiled for Anna-Marie's picture, feeling good that she was interested in me. Because I was interested in her. Her fingernails. Her whole-face smile.

"This is so cute."

She thought I was cute. I smiled at her. I thought she was cute too.

"The phone," she clarified. Not me. "Look how *small* it is. It's like a little baby phone. You know," she said, still laughing, "my nana has a flip phone too. You guys should hang out together. You can send each other predictive text messages, and read books with giant print." Now Anna-Marie's laughter was getting the best of her. "You guys could go out to dinner at four o'clock and read the menu through magnifying glasses and, like, talk about knitting patterns."

I was aware that I was being made fun of. I should have been upset. But I wasn't. I was ready to hang out with Anna-Marie's nana. I would absolutely go out to dinner with her nana, so long as it was a kosher restaurant. I'd make sure to brush up on my knitting, so our conversation would flow. Hopefully Anna-Marie would come too, and she could mock me incessantly while I sweated through layer after layer of clothing.

"Awesome," I said. "Tell her to give me a call."

Anna-Marie just waved goodbye. I watched Borneo drag

her down the block. She disappeared around the corner onto Rhyd Lane.

"Yehuda."

I looked up to see Rabbi Moritz. Usually when a kid went for a walk during school it meant he had a worry or concern on his mind. If he didn't come back quickly, a rabbi would follow and make sure everything was all right, or if there was something the student needed to talk about. I guess I'd been out awhile

"Hi, Rebbe. This is a particularly interesting tree, don't you agree? It's on my short list for best neighborhood tree."

"Are you all right, Yehuda?"

"Fine."

"Something on your mind?" Moritz asked.

There was exactly one thing on my mind, so I said nothing.

"I thought Moshe Tzvi was just kidding about hitting you over the head."

"Do you know where Borneo is, Rebbe?" I asked him.

"No," he said.

"The ocean," I told him. "It's an island. The ocean is where the islands are."

"Come," said Rabbi Moritz. "It's time to pray. Let's walk back to school, and you can tell me about the trees on your list."

I turned and followed him back down the road.

Back at school we had Mincha, afternoon prayers. I went into the beis medrash and took my place next to Moshe Tzvi. As always, he prayed more intensely than anyone else, bowing up and down, the fringes of his blue-and-white tzitzis dancing from their spot at his waist, his prayer book pressed up against his nose.

But I could barely get into the prayers at all. I tried to focus on the Aleinu, recognizing my God, but I almost forgot to bow. And I completely missed the spitting that Moshe Tzvi and I always synchronize.

We don't spit for real because the beis medrash is carpeted. But we all make a spitting sound, a kind of "pthh" with the tongue against the top front teeth. The idea is to protest Christian censorship of Jewish prayer by spitting at a certain point in the recitation. Old synagogues used to have special spittoons just for that purpose, which is pretty cool, because "spittoon" is an awesome word, and because there should probably just be spittoons everywhere.

Moshe Tzvi had spit for real a few times, big old wads of saliva right on the carpet by his feet. He didn't get in trouble. You can't get in trouble for *over*piety. You could sacrifice a goat for Passover, and the rabbis would say, as the blood pooled at their feet, as the animal's dying legs gave a final shuddering kick, "Well, the boy has dedication."

It wasn't the cleanup that stopped Moshe Tzvi's spitting. It was when the kids around him started spitting on his feet that Moshe Tzvi thought better of it. His official justification was, "If we view the spitting as a repudiation of the unbeliever's vanity, then I can justify it, but if we see it simply as a protest of medieval persecution, then its foundation is in secular tradition, rather than in Jewish law itself, in which case the transmutation to mere pantomime is acceptable. I believe it was Rabbi Ismar Elbogen who said—"

"Are you sure it's not just because you have Reuven's spit on your shoes?" I asked him.

"Pretty sure," said Moshe Tzvi.

"Certain?"

"What is certain, Hoodie?" he asked.

As Mincha ended, I hung my fedora on its designated hook and walked out of the beis medrash, into the sunlight. I had to go back into the main building for class, but I was certain I wouldn't learn anything for the rest of that day.

CHAPTER 2

in which I introduce you to my family

FOR OBVIOUS REASONS, YOU CAN'T actually *meet* my family. I'm just going to talk about them. Let's start with me. I'm a member of my family.

Most people call me Hoodie, which is a nickname. My first name is Yehuda, which is the Hebrew version of Judah, son of Jacob. He is best known for jealously casting his brother Joseph into a pit. But I don't have a brother, so there's nothing to worry about as far as fraternal pit-casting is concerned.

My last name is Rosen.

You may have pictured me in your mind. If you're going by grossly exaggerated Jewish stereotypes, then you're spot-on. Mazel tov. I'm a walking bar mitzvah: dark curly hair and a rather prominent nose. I'm thin, and about average height. And though I'm not quick, I have a pretty smooth lefty jump shot. On the JV team, only Chaim Abramowitz is a more consistent shooter.

We're the only sophomores who get to practice with varsity.

I think the only way I break stereotypes is that I don't wear long side curls. My family is Orthodox. Pretty observant. Frum. But we're not Chasidic, so there are some things we get to choose. My dad keeps his sideburns short, and so do I.

You may have pictured my family in your mind. If you're going by grossly exaggerated Orthodox stereotypes, then you're spot-on. Mazel tov. We can only fit in our Honda Odyssey if we lay Chana down across our laps, and undoubtedly my parents are working on populating a second minivan as we speak.

Like most Orthodox schools, my yeshiva has double days. In the morning we have Judaic studies, where we study Torah, the Hebrew bible. In the afternoon we have general studies, where we learn things like history and math. We don't get out of school until just after six in the evening.

That day, I was going to walk right home after school for supper, but I had a text from my older sister, Zippy, saying Dad was held up at work, and the family wouldn't be eating together. Or that's what I understood from it. The text actually said: Dad staring at dirt. Eat yourself.

Zippy is funny.

I'll start with my right arm so I can still text you back, I sent in reply.

The construction site was only a short detour on the route home from school, so I stopped there on the way. Zippy is basically omniscient, because sure enough, my father stood at the edge of the site, staring at a big mound of dirt.

My family, and our Orthodox community, used to live in a town called Colwyn. But then Colwyn became too expensive for a lot of the community families. So some of us moved to Tregaron, where we opened a new school, and a new synagogue.

My family didn't move because of money. We moved because my father works for the development company that was building—or was *trying* to build—an apartment high-rise for families who wanted to join us.

When the decision was made to move some of the community to Tregaron, my dad's company bought a big building next to the commuter train station. The building had been a movie theater, but it had closed years ago and had sat abandoned.

My dad's company demolished the theater. Where it once stood, there was now an enormous expanse of dirt, sand-colored, like a small desert.

My dad stood looking at a dirt mound next to an idle piece of construction equipment. The sun was beginning to set, but still it reflected brightly off the yellow excavator. "Their bigotry is boundless," he said. "They're craven, Yehuda. They're blinded by their hatred of us. We fight the same battle, over and over, generation after generation, millennium after millennium."

Ever since we opened the yeshiva, and my father's company bought the theater, the locals had been trying to stop us from moving here. They talked about us like we were an invading army, like we were going to ride in on horseback with torches and pitchforks, to set their buildings on fire and slaughter them kosher-style. In the online newspaper, they said we would ruin their "way of life," like we were going to go home to home rounding up their bacon, confiscating their shellfish, systematically removing their car batteries on Friday afternoons so they couldn't drive on Shabbos. The woman who rented us our house received threats from neighbors.

"When there's fear like this, fear of us, I know what happens," he said. "It's what happened to your great-grandparents in Ukraine. It's what's happening in Brooklyn."

In Ukraine, pogroms had swept through my great-grandparents' shtetl town. The Russians had killed many of the Jewish men and forced the survivors into armed service. My great-grandfather had cut off his own toes to avoid military conscription. In Brooklyn, recently, there had been attacks on Jews. But those things weren't going to happen here. This wasn't the old country. If I was going to lose my toes, it would be in a freak accident. This wasn't New York City either. Tregaron was a sleepy, quiet town. The locals weren't going to attack us.

"It's always the same," my father repeated. "Always the same."

I'd heard my father give this speech before, but his words always carried a hopeful tone. Now he sounded different. He wasn't staring at his dirt in triumph, imagining all of the Jewish families eating around their Shabbos tables, cooking in their double-fridged kosher kitchens, spitting into their shiny new spittoons. He stared in defeat, seeing only the dirt itself. "We were going to start construction today," my father said. "But they held an emergency town council meeting last night. At ten p.m. they held a meeting. To change the zoning laws they held a ten p.m. meeting. The law now says that this lot can only be commercial. No residences."

My father scratched his beard, but not in a thoughtful way. He suddenly looked old. He'd just turned forty, but his beard was graying, and his eyes looked droopy and tired. "It's that *woman*," he said.

I looked around for a woman, but we were the only two people who'd congregated to watch the sun set over the empty lot. "What woman?"

"Diaz-O'Leary," he said.

Monica Diaz-O'Leary was the mayor of the town. She was leading the charge against us. She'd written an article in the online newspaper, and she'd organized the lawn sign campaign. The lawn signs said, PROTECT TREGARON'S CHARACTER. SAY "NO" TO DEVELOPMENT.

Our next-door neighbors had two of them.

"So what now?" I asked.

"Well, we could get our people onto the town council and overturn the decision, but first we'd have to have enough residents in town to vote, and we can't do that until we build, and we can't build until we change the council. So, I don't know. We'll start with legal action."

"I'm with you. But I'm also *very* hungry. Can supper precede legal action?"

I started the walk home, leaving my father to his dirt. I only made it as far as the kosher market, where my hunger compelled me to go inside and buy Starburst. The kosher market was the only Jewish-owned business in town. It had opened in anticipation of the apartment building. Chaim Abramowitz's family owned it, and he worked there after school.

American Starburst aren't kosher, but British ones are, and the store imported them from England.

At the end of the town's main strip, I crossed the tracks and cut through the cemetery that separated the town's business strip from its biggest residential area. I walked through it every day on my way to and from school, but I never really looked around. Tonight, as I walked by the gravestones, I glanced at their names. A lot of them were Irish-sounding: Quinn, Flanagan, O'Neil. But there was also a Bernier, a Lopez, an Olivieri—it was a real who's who of dead people.

Near the dead Olivieri, I found an equally deceased Chonofsky. It was getting dark, but I could just make out the full name: Miriam Chonofsky. There was no doubt: dead Jew. I smiled at her, my predecessor.

As I walked the final turn of the graveyard's winding path, I noticed a Cohen and a Canter. There was something else I didn't notice, either because it was dark, or because the final setting of the sun marked the end of Tu B'Av, and brought my mind back around to Anna-Marie, and her painted nails, and the way her cross danced around the collar of her T-shirt.

Before I even got to the front door, I was welcomed home by a falling box that hit me on the shoulder. "Hi, Chana," I said.

I have numerous and various sisters. Chana is one of them. She'd recently discovered that she could access the roof through her bedroom window, and her new favorite activity was to stand up there and throw medium-size objects at passersby. She'd started with heavier things: balls, books. I still had a bruise on my arm from the stapler she'd gotten me with the week before. But she'd recently discovered, thank God, that lighter, irregularly shaped projectiles, like Amazon boxes, presented a greater challenge for the rooftop sniper.

"It's good to see you too. How was your day?" I asked, looking up into the dark. Before my eyes could adjust, they were covered when a large box hit me on the temple, bounced back up, then settled over my head. "Nice shot," I told the inside of the box.

"Thanks," said a muffled Chana from above.

In the foyer, I tossed my backpack onto the floor, picked my way through a minefield of toys and books, and stumbled into the kitchen. Zippy was seated at the kitchen table. Zippy was always at the kitchen table. The rest of us—me, my parents, my non-Zippy sisters, even the house itself—we were all planets orbiting around Zippy, our sun, who always sat at the kitchen table.

I could hear some miscellaneous sisters crashing and banging around upstairs. I could hear—or, rather, not hear—the silence of my mother grading exams or lesson-planning in her bedroom. I could hear my stomach growling. But none of it had any effect on Zippy. It never did. Zippy sat at the table with a computer, a stack of papers,

20

and a cup of coffee. She wore a long black skirt, and a denim button-up shirt. Its collar was askew where it met her braided hair.

I approached the counter and stood between our two panini presses, looking back and forth at them, trying to decide. "Which of you wants to join me tonight on my journey to satiation?" I asked them. "Will it be you, dairy press, on an odyssey of cheese? Or will this be a quest of the flesh, dearest meat press?"

"It will be an odyssey of the—no, I'm not going to say it. It'll be dairy," Zippy said.

"Nobody asked you," I told her as I looked through the fridge. "I specifically addressed my inquiry to—"

"We're out of lunch meat. Goldie ate the last slices of turkey."

I said the proper blessing as I washed my hands. Then I loaded up two slices of bread with cheese, and pressed them. I tossed the hot sandwich onto a paper towel, and said the blessing over the bread, though I think you could argue that my meal was almost entirely cheese, at least from a caloric perspective.

We've got blessings for everything. There would definitely be a blessing over the panini press if they'd had biblical paninis. But that was in the pre-panini era. Those had to be rough times for the Jews, wandering in the desert without a toasted sandwich anywhere in sight.

I ate at the counter. Zippy monopolized the table, and there wasn't anywhere to put my food.

"How was school?" Zippy asked without looking up. She was scrolling through something on the computer screen and cross-referencing it with numbers on one of her papers.

My heart skipped a beat. She wouldn't have asked the question if she didn't already know something. Had she run into one of my rabbis? Had somebody seen me talking to Anna-Marie?

"It was . . . fine," I offered.

"I ask," she went on, "because we got an email from Rabbi Moritz, saying that you're *already* failing math and Gemara."

The email had certainly been sent to my parents, but who knows when they would have gotten around to reading it. They might never have looked at it. Zippy was late-teens-ish—I could calculate her exact age, but as we've established, I'm bad at math—and she took care of those kinds of things, fielding the school emails and phone calls from her table office.

"Instead of being disappointed, I feel like you should try being impressed."

"That's fair," she said. "It is impressive that in only two weeks you're already failing to the point where the rabbi feels the need to send a note home." Still, she didn't sound impressed, or amused. Zippy took this kind of thing personally, especially since math and scripture were her things. She'd graduated high school the year before, and she was taking college classes to be an engineer. When she spoke again, she sounded tired and resigned. "How did the apple fall so far from the tree?" she asked.

I chewed some toasty crust. "You're not the tree. You're just another apple. It's more like, how did the same tree produce a crisp, shiny apple, but then a rotten, misshapen, worm-eaten apple?"

"You're not rotten or misshapen," Zippy said, so at least she agreed I was worm-eaten. "What are you even doing this year?

Geometry? I know it's a struggle for you, but . . . *already?*"

"Math is from the sitra achra."

"Everything you don't like is from 'the other side.'"

"I'm sorry. I must have misspoken. I meant to say, Zippy, my dear elder sister, that math is great. Will you teach me?"

"Don't bother with the math. You're a Jewish boy. Nobody cares if you can do math. Let's focus on the Gemara. A Jewish boy has to know Talmud."

She looked up from her computer, and we made eye contact for the first time. Zippy's eyes were dark and deep-set like mine. Looking at her was a lot like looking at myself, if I were older, smarter, wiser, and female.

Sometimes I wished we could swap.

I was stuck as the only boy in the family, with all the expectations that role carried with it. I never met those expectations: I didn't do well in school. I couldn't offer a decent Talmud interpretation to save my life. I could barely read Hebrew. Meanwhile, Zippy didn't *have* to clear any high bars, but she did so with ease. She could quote obscure religious commentary, or create computer-assisted designs by expending the same amount of mental energy it took me to, say, put on socks.

There was a crash above our heads, followed by a thump that shook the ceiling. It sounded like a Goldie thump, but Zippy overruled me. "That was Rivkie," she said. "You can tell by the way the chandelier is shaking." Her hypothesis was confirmed, because the ensuing cries were distinctly Rivkian, ambulance-like wails only she could produce. "I'll tell you what. I'll work with you on your Gemara *if* you take care of that," and Zippy indicated the ceiling with her pen.

"And I'll take care of that *if* you make me two more paninis."

"No."

"It was worth a try."

I walked over to the table and left my paper towel there, then went upstairs to coo over Rivkie's bruise.

CHAPTER 3

in which we discuss livestock and the differentiation therebetween

MOSHE TZVI GUTMAN IS A polarizing figure. I'm polarized by him. On the one hand, I don't like him, because he's not a very nice person, and he's crude and embarrassing to be around, and he has trouble picking up basic social cues, and he has a superior attitude about just about everything, which is ill-fitting because there really isn't much that he's good at, outside of Talmud study.

On the other hand, he's my best friend in the world. Are you supposed to *like* your friends? I don't think that's how friendship works. I don't particularly like Moshe Tzvi, and I've never thought about whether he likes me, but I know that Moshe Tzvi would do *anything* for me. He would literally kill somebody for me. He's told me that many times, actually. He seems pretty eager to kill somebody on my behalf. He's real into weapons and violence. "You just say the word, Hoodie," he tells me. Before he does his rabbinical training, he wants to join the army.

Today he was wearing his Israel Defense Forces T-shirt.

T-shirts are against the dress code, but the rabbis will overlook just about any dress code violation if your outfit has a Jewish star on it. You could probably come to school in a Speedo if it had an Israeli flag on the back.

Moshe Tzvi was also wearing mittens. He claimed that he'd slept in them, and nobody doubted it. The right one was soaked in milk—it's tough to eat cereal in mittens.

Following up on our morning hand-washing lesson from the day before, Rabbi Moritz was talking about the other stuff we must do to start the day. "The procedures are clear," he said. "So what are the commentaries focused on in their treatment of the subject?"

I looked at the commentaries on the outer edge of the page, but I couldn't get the words to come together for me. My heart was still racing from my morning walk to school.

Nobody seemed to have the answer. Even Moshe Tzvi was silent.

"The question they are forced to ask . . ." Rabbi Moritz's voice climbed and "ask" came out in pure falsetto. "Sure, we can know what we must do when the day begins. This we can know easily. But it isn't useful if we don't know *when* the day begins."

Heads around the classroom nodded.

"So. According to the medieval commentaries, when does the day begin?"

I watched Moshe Tzvi's left mitten trace over the text, as his right mitten rose into the air.

Rabbi Moritz recognized him, and leaned forward over the desk at the front of the room.

"The day begins," Moshe Tzvi said, "when there is enough light to distinguish between an ass and a wild ass."

That's the thing about Moshe Tzvi's Talmud interpretation: It's always vaguely inappropriate, but it's also always correct, so it's tough for the rabbis to get him in trouble. When I really focused on the page, I could see that he was spot-on. The medieval commentaries agreed that the day began when you could tell the difference between a domestic animal and a wild one.

"It's about if you can distinguish between different types of asses," Moshe Tzvi explained, indicating a passage in the book with his thumb. "That's what it says. It's about ass differentiation. Perception of ass, you could say. It's all about ass: the ass that you *can* see and the ass that you, despite your *attempt* to see the ass, cannot—"

Rabbi Moritz cleared his throat and readjusted his tie. "Most scholars translate it as 'donkey.' In fact, if you look at your—"

"Most? But not all? So you're saying, Rebbe, that there are ass rabbis? There are just fewer of them? It's a small but proud group, the ass rabbinate?"

"Don't push it, Moshe Tzvi. What you say is right, but don't cross the line to profanity, to nivul peh."

"May I push it just a *bit* further? Because I would like your blessing to be an ass student, Rebbe."

Rabbi Moritz clenched his mouth shut and stared at Moshe Tzvi.

"Blessing denied," said Reuven.

"The rebbe rises at the rim," I said, imitating a sports

announcer, "and *slams* the blessing right back in Gutman's face. The crowd goes—"

Moritz cut me off when he started yelling. "Why are my fingers straight?" he shouted. The spit on his upper lip launched itself across his desk. "Why? Why? The Gemara says my fingers are straight. Why!?" He was hollering at us now.

The rabbi looked at each of us in turn, his eyes digging into ours. One by one we shook our heads.

Of course Moshe Tzvi was the only one who knew. Moshe Tzvi's blue eyes shone when Moritz turned to him. He gave the rabbi a friendly wave of his mitten.

"What then, Moshe Tzvi?"

"I am prepared to answer your question, Rebbe, but only if you give me your ass blessing."

Talmud discussion is always like this: warlike. It is a battle of wits, knowledge, and, in this case, wills. I think it's always been like that.

Jewish tradition is based around Torah. There are two Torahs. God gave one of them to Moses on Mount Sinai. That's the Written Torah, and it was presented to Moses freshly printed and collated. The other Torah is the Oral Torah. I guess God didn't have enough time to write it down—dude is busy—so he just kind of whispered it to Moses as a P.S. Moses, who left Egypt without his laptop charger, didn't have the chance to type it up. So he just told people about it. And then those people told other people about it, and it was passed on orally from generation to generation, which, if you ask me, is not the best way to preserve indispensable knowledge from God himself.

Nobody did ask me, but some Babylonian rabbis had the same idea, and they wrote all the stuff down. They transcribed it from memory in a combination of Aramaic and Ancient Hebrew, without punctuation. Because it's based on old stories these guys' dads told them, written in a combination of antiquated languages, and missing all of its semicolons, it is a confusing document.

For two thousand years, various rabbis tried to make sense of it, and they wrote down their commentaries, arguments, and contradictions, and attached them to the original document. These attachments are called the Gemara. The original Oral Torah plus all these commentaries make up the Talmud. It's a giant maze of Jewish laws, rules, thoughts, considerations, ruminations. Studying it is, as Moshe Tzvi once put it, "basically medieval torture, but the cool, Jewish kind. It hurts so good."

In school, we study Talmud every day.

In this battle of wills, Rabbi Moritz won. "Why?" he asked one final time. "Why, Moshe Tzvi?"

Moshe Tzvi peeled off his right mitten slowly and dramatically, then flexed long slender fingers. "The Gemara says that my fingers are straight so that if I hear nivul peh, I can put my fingers in my ears to shut it out."

"Amazing," said Rabbi Moritz. And as with any Talmud battle, as soon as it was resolved, the combatants were friends once again. The rebbe nodded to Moshe Tzvi, reopened his book, and turned the page forward.

In my mind, I flipped the page the other way, back to my deeply unnerving walk to school. My heart rate was still elevated, and my legs still felt a little jiggly. I had thought the routine of normal class would settle me down, but I was wrong.

I'd woken up that day when my alarm went off. My alarm is Zippy's foot. There are dents and scuffs at the bottom of my bedroom door from Zippy's morning kicks, because she always has too many items and/or sisters in her arms to knock with her hand.

Even if the front lawn had been packed with livestock, it would have been too dark to see them clearly. I said the Modeh Ani, got out of bed, washed my hands, ate five to seven granola bars, and hustled out the door.

I walked to school in the same half-asleep trance I did every morning, staring at my feet, willing them to keep moving.

Do you believe in coincidences? The Torah says that coincidences don't exist, that God has his hand in everything. That's fine. But then, how detail-oriented is the guy? I get he would care if I violated one of his commandments. But where's the line? Does he mind if I jaywalk? Does he care if my socks match?

I ask because after I put magical Band-Aids on Rivkie's bruised knee, told Goldie to be more careful when she pushed people off of ledges, checked that Chana and Leah were at least pretending to do their homework, and ate several more paninis, I'd spent the rest of the previous evening thinking about Anna-Marie, running our short conversation through my head on repeat, picturing me and her (and her nana) sharing a meal together, wishing that when she'd reached out her hand to shake, I'd taken it. In the light that shone into my bedroom from the street, I'd stared at my hand, trying to imagine what hers would have felt like in mine.

Then, as I walked to school just after sunrise, I wondered what she was doing at the same time. That's what I was wondering right up until I saw what she was doing.

I had just entered the cemetery when I saw her. I threw on the brakes. The cemetery was quiet and still in the muggy morning air.

Anna-Marie's attire was sparse again, with exposed arms and legs. In my community, we've got this thing called tznius, rules of modesty that she was breaking in like eight different ways. She was wearing a kind of tunic, except the bottom wasn't a skirt. Just below her waist, it split into wide billowy shorts. She was wearing the same sneakers, but her dark black hair was down this time, falling just below her shoulders where it ended in a straight line across the top of her back.

Even from a distance I could tell she was crying, which I guess wasn't surprising—crying is one of the more popular cemetery activities. She was standing in front of one of the newer-looking headstones, looking down at it. Every moment or so, a tear would dangle off her chin and drop into the grass.

My first instinct was to hide behind a headstone. I was about to dive behind one, but then I thought to myself: How do I best go about *not* looking like a serial killer? Peering at somebody creepily from behind a gravestone didn't seem like the best choice.

So I decided I'd just walk through the cemetery like a normal person walking through a cemetery. People walked through cemeteries all the time. I could just be one of those people.

The only walking path took me right by her. I tried to keep my eyes down at my feet. But a kid only has so much willpower. So when she glanced up, we made eye contact.

I saw her recognize me, and she smiled at me through her tears. I spontaneously combusted and subsequently ceased to exist.

Not really. That's what I expected to happen. But actually she said, "Hey, it's you."

"Yeah," I said, agreeing that I was me.

"Hoodie."

"Yep. Anna-Marie."

"Nice," she said, and then she went about straightening her already-straight clothing, pulling at one of her sleeves.

Something about the way she wasn't quite looking me in the eye put me at ease. Talking to her the day before, despite all my heavy clothing, I'd felt exposed. Anna-Marie had a poise and self-confidence I couldn't match, and it had made me feel vulnerable. But now *she* seemed vulnerable. I hadn't meant to catch her in this kind of personal moment, but I was glad I did, because suddenly she wasn't quite as terrifying. She wasn't some kind of angelic apparition. She was a human person, just like me.

"Where's Borneo?" I asked.

"This is his grave," she replied.

"Oh, I—"

"Jesus, that's not true. I can't believe I said that. I'm horrible. Jesus Christ. I'm sorry. Are you here to . . . see somebody?"

"No. It's just the fastest way to get to school. My family isn't from around here, originally. You know," I finished, as a reference to my outsider status: my dress shirt, my kippah, the lawn signs. But maybe Anna-Marie didn't know about the lawn signs. You probably only paid attention to them if they were directed at you.

"Right," she said. "My family—well, most of them—have been here for forever. My great-grandparents are buried here too."

When she'd joked that it was Borneo's grave, my eyes had instinctively shot over to the gravestone Anna-Marie was standing over. But my eyes hadn't immediately focused on it—they don't usually do the focus thing until ten a.m. at the earliest. But now they did focus.

The last name was O'Leary. First name Kevin. I looked at the dates listed under his name and did some light math. He'd died this year at fortyish, just the right age for him to be Anna-Marie's father.

"Is—was that—"

"My dad? Yeah." Anna-Marie had stopped crying but still she wiped at her eyes.

"Crap," I said.

"Yeah," she agreed. "It *really* sucks."

But we weren't talking about the same thing. I wish I could say my nivul peh was about her father's death. But it wasn't. It was about the fact that her father was O'Leary, which made her

(Diaz-)O'Leary, which made her mom Diaz-O'Leary, which made her mom the mayor, the one who'd stopped the apartment building's construction, who was trying to keep us out of Tregaron.

I didn't know what to say, so I said what any good Jewish boy was taught to say, "Zichrono livracha." And when Anna-Marie gave me a weird look, I translated, "May his memory be a blessing."

"Yeah," she said, "a blessing." And she started walking. I was going to just wait there for her to go away, but she said, "Come on," and I caught up to her.

"Do you like it here?" she asked.

"Yeah, I mean, it's a fine cemetery."

"No. You know, the town. Tregaron."

Honestly, I hadn't really thought about it. I wasn't given a choice about moving here. Enough of my friends and classmates had come with me that it didn't feel so different.

"I like it okay," I said. "But the town doesn't like—"

Anna-Marie cut me off with a yelp, a sudden, sharp intake of breath.

I looked where she was looking, down near our feet. Next to her blue-striped Adidas sneaker was the Cohen I'd noticed the night before. His name was Oscar Cohen. He'd died in the late 1940s.

But now I noticed there was a swastika on his gravestone. It was done in black spray paint. The center of the Nazi symbol hovered above his name, and the bottom-right arm reached toward his dates. There was another swastika on the nearby Elsie Cantor gravestone, about the same size, also black. The Cantor headstone was bigger, and it left room for some additional commentary: *Go home, Jews,* it said.

I tried to process what I was looking at. The message on the Cantor grave was talking to me directly, telling me to go away, that I was unwanted, rejected by the place that was supposed to be my new home.

I'd been aware of antisemitism my whole life, but I'd never *faced* it. Now I was literally staring it in the face. Or, I should have been.

But instead of looking at the graffiti, I looked at Anna-Marie. Her eyes were wide as she stared at the gravestones. She was frozen still, as in a photograph. Somehow I could tell that she wanted to look at me, but was forcing herself not to.

Slowly she turned her head to me. "I—" she began.

"It's okay," I said.

"It's *not* okay."

"Of course it's not okay. That's not what I meant. I meant, it's okay. Let's just go." I didn't want to look at it anymore. I didn't want my interaction with Anna-Marie to be ruined by this. But it was too late for that.

We walked in silence. The silence was uncomfortable. It wrapped around us like a kind of fog. It was constricting.

Both of us wanted to split up, but neither of us wanted to be the one to go our own way. I took all of the normal streets to school, hoping with each turn that her house would be in a different direction. But her house was half a block from the school, directly on my usual route.

When we got there, Anna-Marie stopped. Behind her, standing tall in her front yard, was one of the lawn signs. The way Anna-Marie was standing, it almost seemed like she was blocking it intentionally, but I couldn't be sure.

I thought she was going to say something, but she didn't. She just turned and went up the front walk.

The house was a colonial with an open porch on the bottom level. A couple thick white columns supported the overhanging second floor. It looked a lot like the one my family rented across town, except this one was in much better shape, and there wasn't anybody on the roof above the porch hurling household objects at the people in the yard.

There was one person in the yard, next to the porch. This was probably the mayor, Monica Diaz-O'Leary. She was wearing a loose shirt and those exercise pants that basically show what you'd look like naked if you dyed your bottom half black. She was holding Borneo's leash, and Borneo was sniffing around in a flower bed.

Mrs. Diaz-O'Leary looked up when her daughter came up the walk. She had to notice I was there on the sidewalk, but she didn't wave or anything. She reached out and put an arm around Anna-Marie, and mother and daughter disappeared into the house.

I was still standing at the curb when Anna-Marie burst back out of the front door. She jogged down the front walk.

"What's your number, Hoodie?" she asked. "I'd just look you up on Insta or TikTok, but . . ." And her voice trailed off.

I looked back and forth between her and her lawn sign. She was one of *them*. Even if she condemned it. I resolved not to give her my number.

I gave her my number. "You can tell your nana she can call before bedtime," I said. "So, like, anytime before eight o'clock."

Anna-Marie laughed nervously. But a nervous laugh was still a laugh.

The laugh made me feel great, and I felt great for the half block to school, where Shacharis, morning prayers, reminded me about the cemetery. When I rocked back and forth, and closed my eyes, I saw the swastikas on the inside of my eyelids. They hovered there, as though projected on a screen, reminding me what they stood for. Millions of Jews had been slaughtered under that symbol, *for* that symbol. That morning, I prayed for their memories.

After prayer, I'd told Rabbi Moritz that I wanted to talk to him about something. I didn't really want to open a can of worms— I'm a firm believer that worms should remain in their cans where they belong—but I didn't know what else to do. I couldn't just let people deface gravestones, and not say anything. What would my ancestors think?

When the rest of the class stampeded out of the room to grab snacks before the next period, I waited behind.

"Yehuda," Rabbi Moritz said, as he organized books on his desk.

I was about to release the worms, but then my phone buzzed in my pocket. Instinctively, I grabbed it and flipped it open. It was a text from a number I didn't know. It said: Hoodie! It's your new friend, Anna-Marie. I feel so bad about the graffiti. Do you want to help me fix it?

Before I'd even processed the message, I sent back, Yes. Now?

I thought you had school, Anna-Marie replied.

Kind of

How do you kind of have school?

I'll explain

Meet me at my ■, she sent. I was pretty sure the box was supposed to be a graphic, but my phone didn't get emojis. I guessed that the emoji was a house.

"Yehuda," Moritz said again. "You said you had something urgent to tell me?"

"Oh, yeah," I said. "I neglected to tell you yesterday about a birch tree that I enjoy a great deal. I was so preoccupied with that oak that I totally blanked. But now I'm . . . busy. I've got to go. We'll have to do this another time."

Moritz slipped a couple books under his arm, squared his shoulders to me, and gave a little bow. "I look forward to hearing all about it at a later date," he said.

"You won't be disappointed," I assured him as I followed him out the door.

I bounded down the stairs to the curb and took long strides toward the Diaz-O'Leary lawn. Borneo came out to greet me, then sprinted back to my new friend, Anna-Marie. My new friend didn't greet me at all. She just matched my stride on the sidewalk and directed us toward town. Borneo trailed behind on his leash.

Anna-Marie was tall, about my height, but she was all limbs. She walked in a kind of lope, with her long legs preceding her, pulling her along like the leash pulled the dog.

"So how do you *kind of* have school? And why are you in school in August?" she asked.

"We have school in August because we miss so many days for holidays the rest of the year. It's a legal thing. And . . ." I paused and tried to think how best to explain that I could just walk out of school anytime I wanted. "Okay, well, what's the point of school?" I asked her.

"To learn science, math, history? To get ready for college? To look at cute boys but pretend you're not looking at them?"

She and I went to *very* different schools. Though maybe she'd like mine. There were *lots* of boys there. "The point of school," I said, "is to become a true man, to learn the right way to live, to learn how to best serve God. That's my type of school anyway. Now that we're men, we need to learn how to find our own relationship with God and with our religion, to understand *why* we live the way we do, why it's *important* to live that way, and sometimes that requires self-reflection, and so if we need to self-reflect, we can take a walk."

"So, that's what you're doing right now, self-reflecting?"

"Yeah," I said. "How self-reflective do I look?"

"*So* self-reflective. You're self-reflection personified, man.

Jesus, if I just left school, they could send the police after me."

"We follow a different set of rules, I guess," I said.

"I've noticed," Anna-Marie said.

"What's *that* mean?" I asked.

Anna-Marie looked at Borneo. "I didn't . . ."

"No. What do you mean?"

"I didn't mean to offend you. I'm sorry."

I wasn't offended. Wait. Yes, I was. Everything about Anna-Marie offended me: the way she dressed, her joke about her father's grave, the lawn sign in her yard. But it's like I was saying about Moshe Tzvi: you don't have to like your friends. I could be deeply offended by Anna-Marie and still want to spend *all* of my time with her.

"I just don't know what you mean," I said.

"You guys—not 'you guys.' I . . . Fine, we're friends, right?"

"Yeah, we're friends," I said, mostly because I wanted to hear myself say it out loud. I wanted to say it over and over again.

"Okay, it's just that sometimes I see—well, your people, I guess—not really paying attention to the real world. Like, there will be a guy just walking across the road without looking at the cars coming, or kids will just walk through people's yards on the way to school or whatever. Our new neighbors . . . If I wake up in the middle of the night, their kids are running around in the yard, shouting at each other, and it's like two in the morning. I'm not—I don't mean to—"

"Huh," I said. I'd never really thought about the first one. Didn't everybody jaywalk? But then I was guilty of the second one. I cut at least two lawns on my way to school every day. And I had to admit that Chana kept watch from her sniper's perch at just about any hour of the day and/or night. "The real world . . ." I wondered. "What is the *real* world?"

"This one," Anna-Marie said, and she indicated the neighborhood, the hot day, the business strip of town we were approaching on foot.

I didn't agree, but I wasn't about to contradict her.

We walked in silence for a minute. Then she said, "Maybe it would be better if there were another world to slip into. This one isn't always so great, is it? At the very least, I'd like there to be another one where I could get away from my mom."

Anna-Marie tied Borneo up outside the little hardware store.

Outside, the late summer sun was oppressive. At least it felt that way to me. But there were still plenty of people out, enjoying the inferno. Young parents pushed little children in strollers. Kids our age popped in and out of the coffee shop sipping iced drinks. Now and then a masochist jogged by, panting like Borneo.

In the hardware store it was cool, and it smelled like sawdust. The woman at the register looked up when we walked in. I never walked into any of the businesses on the downtown strip, except for the kosher market, because of the way the people looked at me when I did. This woman wasn't giving me a mean look or anything. It was just a reflexive raise of the eyebrows that asked, "What's *he* doing in here?" As though Jewish nuts and bolts were different from gentile ones.

The woman's expression changed when she saw my friend.

"Anna-Marie," she said. "To what do I owe the pleasure?"

I'm a very bad liar. I'm just spectacularly bad at it. I would have trouble telling you, for example, that I like zucchini.

I *love* zucchini. It's delicious. I particularly enjoy how . . . squashy it is.

No. That's not true. I hate zucchini. It's gross.

See what I'm saying?

So I was surprised by the ease with which Anna-Marie lied to the hardware lady. "Just running an errand for my ma," she said.

"And how is she?" the hardware lady asked with an air of concern.

"Fine. Fine."

"What can we help you with?"

Anna-Marie approached the counter. I lurked behind her, swaying forward, then back, then forward, slowly.

Anna-Marie turned her phone around to face the lady at the counter. "I don't know exactly what she needs it for, but she said to get something like this. To get spray paint off."

The woman slipped nimbly around the counter and started walking toward the back of the store.

We followed.

The woman plucked a bottle off the shelf and handed it to Anna-Marie. "This should do," she said. "You'll just need a few rags."

"Do you sell them?"

"What? Rags? The mayor doesn't have rags?"

"I don't know. I don't want her to send me back."

"I'll grab you a couple pads—they should work. I'll meet

42

you at the counter."

Anna-Marie paid, assured the lady that she would say hi to her mom for her, and then we were back out on the street with Borneo, heading toward the cemetery. We took a weird route, going away from the main strip, looping around. "*Everybody* knows me here," Anna-Marie explained.

That was true. The lady at the hardware store knew her by name, and even on the side streets, off the main drag, everybody waved when she passed.

I'd known that feeling back in Colwyn. Everybody there had been Jewish, and everybody knew me and my family. And they would stop and ask me how my parents were, and tell me that they'd just seen Zippy and Yoel at the Judaica store (and how happy the couple had been together), and how I looked "more and more like [my] father every day."

When I walked around Tregaron, nobody looked at me. When we first moved, I didn't mind the anonymity, but now, with the graffiti, their downcast eyes felt more sinister. It was as though they actively avoided looking at me, like they preferred to pretend I wasn't there.

"I can't wait to get out of here," Anna-Marie said. "I'm going to go to NYU, the biggest school in the biggest city, where nobody knows me. I want to see if I can never run into the same person twice."

We took a side entrance into the cemetery and headed straight for Cohen and Cantor. The swastikas stood out more starkly in the bright light of midday.

Anna-Marie squatted down and unpacked the paper bag. I

bent down next to her as she placed the bottle and the pads on the ground in front of the gravestones. We were close: me, her, the defaced graves. She reached out and put her hand on my arm. I had my long-sleeve shirt rolled up just a little, and one of her fingers touched my bare skin. It was strange how normal it felt, how something so strange, something almost unthinkable, could feel just like anything else. It was the kind of moment in which you'd expect thunder, an eruption of brimstone, some kind of sign from God. You'd expect Mr. Cohen to rise from his grave and yell at me in Yiddish.

But nothing like that happened. I smiled inwardly and Anna-Marie said, "I'm really sorry, Hoodie. People are awful. I can't imagine how I'd feel if somebody did this to my . . ."

And then, instead of holding her hand on my arm for all eternity as I'd hoped she would, she unscrewed the bottle and we got to work.

I had to admit that this was not how I'd pictured my first ever date going. I couldn't decide which part was more unlikely: the girl who wasn't Jewish, or the activity, which was painstakingly erasing antisemitic graffiti from gravestones.

"Erasing" wasn't the right word choice. "Smearing" was more accurate.

"I'm sorry about what's happening," Anna-Marie said, dabbing some more paint remover on her pad. "I think it's just how old people are. They don't like change. Tregaron's kind of been the same way for a really long time. Everybody knows everybody. Everybody went to the same schools, and they've been shopping at the same old stores. They don't want it to change."

"Things do change, though," I said.

"Says the kid with the flip phone."

"I don't *want* to have a—" I began, then stopped. "It's to protect me from—" But I didn't want to finish that sentence either. The flip phone was to protect me from getting distracted from Torah, to keep me from spending my time watching videos, or viewing memes, or looking up pictures of girls dressed like the one who'd just touched me. "It feels different, though. If it weren't . . . us, it would be different. People talk about it like we're an invading army."

"But aren't you? In a way?"

"We're not trying to *pillage*. We just want to find a place to live."

"Maybe I'm only hearing what my ma tells me," Anna-Marie said, "but if you guys build that high-rise, won't the town have *twice* as many people? Won't everything be different then?"

That was probably true. That was the goal: remake the town with Jewish stores, kosher restaurants, a new synagogue and study center, an eruv, businesses closed on Shabbos.

"I don't think old people did this, though," I said about the graffiti.

"Yeah. It was probably kids. They'll probably brag about it on social media. When I said, 'People are awful,' I meant *all* people."

By the time the sweat was beading on our chins, neither

the swastikas nor the message on the Cantor grave was recognizable. It just looked like somebody had dumped some particularly dark mud on the headstones. I stopped for a moment, checked the time on my phone, and did a double take. "I have to go," I said.

"We're almost done," Anna-Marie said.

"I—I have to. I'll miss Mincha. Prayers. You can miss pretty much the whole day. You could skip math class the *entire* year, and I plan to. But if you miss prayers, they take you back behind the woodshed and beat you with the belt of Jewish guilt."

Anna-Marie wiped her brow and looked at me out of the tops of her eyes.

"It's a figurative woodshed," I clarified. "We don't have a real woodshed. Or a belt."

"Oh."

"I'll get in a lot of trouble, is what I'm saying."

"I get it. Should I finish up?"

"Yeah." I stood up and stretched my legs. Out of the corner of my eye I thought I saw somebody near the entrance of the cemetery, a figure in a dark suit with a hat. But it might have just been my guilty conscience, because when I looked again, there was nothing there.

"Should we do this again?" Anna-Marie asked, then corrected herself. "Not *this*. You know what I mean. Hang out."

I didn't want to smile at her. I wanted to act chill, like hanging out with cool gentile girls was just a normal thing I did. But I was beaming. I couldn't make my mouth close. I nodded a bunch and started my power walk back to school.

I got back late, dripping sweat. I slipped into my spot next to Moshe Tzvi and prayed Mincha. Rabbi Friedman led the prayers, calling out in his usual singsong. He had a quiet, peaceful tone that made you forget the outside world, and the modular building you were standing in.

I felt at peace, swaying back and forth, thinking about Anna-Marie. I was still unsettled about the graffiti, but I felt good about fixing it. And I could still feel her fingers on my arm, a touch that marked me as her friend. No, it was more than that. A girl didn't just touch a guy if there wasn't something more than friendship going on.

Near the end of the service, I noticed Rabbi Moritz stealing the occasional glance at me, and he approached me in the bottleneck as we all waited to exit the beis medrash. "Meet me in my office," he said.

"I have class."

"It wasn't a request."

Now that I actually looked at him, I could see that he was angry. And sweaty. My math is bad, but I put two and two together.

Before the yeshiva bought the land the year before, the main building had been a Presbyterian church. I didn't know much about Presbyterians. I only knew they were Christians because Jesus was all over the building: on the stained glass, in the carvings above the main doors.

I'm pretty sure Moritz's office had been a closet when the

school was a church. The yeshiva's rabbis had little makeshift offices scattered all over the school. Moritz's was windowless, and the door hit his desk every time it opened. The walls were unadorned, save for a portrait of the Chofetz Chaim on the wall.

"Would you like a seltzer?" Rabbi Moritz asked me.

Moritz kept a little fridge under his desk, and he always offered you a seltzer when he met with you. If somebody saw you walking around the school with a can of seltzer, they'd ask you, "What'd you do?" because the seltzer told them you were in trouble.

"It's awfully hot out there," the rabbi said. "The seltzer is cold."

I said nothing. It was always best to let the rabbi make the first move. Maybe he was only upset that I'd been late to Mincha.

But the rebbe said nothing. He bent down and opened the fridge door. He carefully selected a can of seltzer. From a slanted shelf at his right, he took a plastic cup, and he poured the seltzer down the side of the cup. The seltzer fizzed. The rabbi took a long sip, staring at me over the rim of the glass.

"I didn't see any birch trees in the cemetery," Moritz said quietly, almost like he was talking to the seltzer.

I really wanted to insist, to the contrary, that the cemetery was *full* of birch trees. The only issue was that I had no idea what a birch tree looked like. "Yes, well, you see, Rebbe, the birch tree is so stunning that it's difficult to remain for any extended duration in its presence. It is best to ponder its splendor from a safe remove, where one can—actually, I will take that seltzer."

"Strawberry?"

"Lime if you have."

"Fine choice."

He slid the seltzer across the desk to me. I popped it open and drank greedily. As I guzzled, I decided that the best course of action was to lie through my teeth. "I was just visiting my grandfather's grave," I told him.

"Zichrono livracha. May he rest in peace. What was his name?"

"Cohen."

"First name?"

I couldn't remember the first name on the grave, but I went with "Moshe," because there was about a one-in-four chance that any given Jewish man was Moshe.

"Which side of the family?" Rabbi Moritz inquired.

"Mother's," I said quickly.

Rabbi Moritz sighed. "Yehuda, I *know* your mother's father. He's *alive.* I saw him at your bar mitzvah two years ago, and again during Purim last spring."

The rebbe's story checked out. I remembered both of those events. I liked my grandpa, even if he had perpetually bad breath. "Well, he has a spot picked out already. You know, one of those family plot kind of deals."

"Do you know what the Talmud says about lying?" Rabbi Moritz asked me.

"It's . . . strongly in favor of it?"

"'Truth is the seal of the Holy One, blessed be He.' *That's*

49

what it says. Rashi explains to us that where there is truth, there is God, and we feel His absence whenever falsehoods are told."

I definitely felt the absence of *something* in the room.

The most compelling reason to learn Talmud was so I could win arguments. But I wasn't going to beat the rebbe. He had an encyclopedic knowledge of Jewish law and had memorized the commentaries of every important Jewish philosopher. The dude had Rashi in one pocket, Ibn Ezra in the other, and Nachmanides lurking in his desk drawer, ready to burst out and crush me with the sheer force of their collective learning.

"There were swastikas on the graves," I said quietly. "I was cleaning them off. And there was a girl there who saw them too. She was helping me. But I didn't do it. I didn't deface Jewish graves."

The rebbe shook his head sadly. "Oh, Yehuda. Oh, Yehuda," he said.

I tried to match his sadness. The graffiti made me sad, and scared. But I also felt proud that Anna-Marie and I had fixed it.

"I almost wish you *had* done it."

"What?" I said. "You wish I'd *defaced* Jewish graves? Why? Because then that would mean we weren't surrounded by anti-semites? It would mean Tregaron didn't hate us, wasn't trying to drive us away as we were driven from—"

"Over the years, I have seen many young Jews internalize the loathing they receive from the outside world. That self-hate can be a difficult affliction to fight against, but it can be overcome. I can help *that* young man back to Torah. But this is something different, these thoughts you're having. These urges, *these* urges, they are stronger."

"These urges? Can you describe them for me, Rebbe?"

"I don't think that would be a productive use of our time."

"I just want to be clear about which urges we're talking about."

"Corporal ones."

"Oh, *now* I understand, because I totally know what that word—"

I got exactly the rise I was looking for. "The *body*, Yehuda. Thoughts and urges relating to the *human body*."

Was I thinking about Anna-Marie's human body? Well, *now* I was. Score one for the rebbe.

"This is why we shelter our students," he went on. "This is why focus, concentration, dedication is so important at your age, because certain distractions are stronger than others. I don't envy you. There are many more distractions today. Distractions such as this make it harder to turn to Torah. But to Torah we must turn. You may think that you can fight antisemitism by engaging with the outside. But you cannot. You believe that if you open yourself up to the outside world, they will accept you. But they won't. We know. We have centuries of evidence. We've seen it over and over. That's why we have to have our own schools, our own businesses. It's the only way. With your fellow Jews, and with HaShem, you will find peace in this life. But HaShem cannot be found in the secular world. Only through Torah can you connect with Him. There's a midrash—I taught it to you—that says that Torah study is the *only* way to overcome our enemies. Do you understand?"

I understood what he was saying: my friendship with Anna-Marie, the enemy, would keep me from Torah, and I couldn't fight antisemitism with a gentile. Except that was what I'd *just* done when we removed the paint.

I finished my seltzer and put the can down on the desk.

Rabbi Moritz was looking through me. "Your people fought and died for the Torah. When it was banned, they studied it in secret, risking their lives, and the lives of their wives and children. You *have* Torah. Every day you are given Torah. You don't have to fight for it. You are given Torah and you do not take it." He put his hands on the desk. "We will help you overcome this. We will guide you back to Torah, Yehuda. After the pogroms, after the inquisition, after the Holocaust, we made ourselves whole again through Torah. Only through Torah will we overcome what we face here in this new place."

He talked about me like I'd come down with some kind of flu, like Anna-Marie had spread to me some kind of goyishe disease. I half expected the rebbe to pull out a piece of paper and write me a prescription for a pill to cure me. He said nothing about the swastikas, or about the fact that I'd done the right thing by removing them.

"I don't see why they have to be two separate things. Why can't I do both of them at the same time?"

"Both of what? Torah and . . . a *girl*?"

I didn't see a point in answering the question.

Now the rebbe was looking directly at me. "You will not leave the school again without permission, Yehuda. In this way, we will help you. If you need to leave school, if you need to take a walk, I will go with you."

"That's great," I said. "Bring your wife. We can double-date."

I didn't mean to say that.

Everything would have been fine if I hadn't said that.

Rabbi Moritz exploded like a grenade, spittle flying across the desk like shrapnel. I didn't hear most of what he said. There was something about disrespect, a question about what my father would think, and something about "kids these days." Nothing about the swastikas.

The office door slammed behind me and I was out in the hall holding my empty can of seltzer, crushed in my clenched fist. A small crowd—enough for a minyan—had formed in the hall. "What'd you do?" Moshe Tzvi asked.

I threw the seltzer can at him.

CHAPTER 4

in which, at the behest of my legal representation, I eat string cheese

AS SOON AS MY LAST class ended, I got a text from Zippy: Run home like your life depends on it because it does. You and your counsel must prepare your defense before dad gets home.

Omniscience was the only way to explain how Zippy knew about this already, but I did as she said. I jogged most of the way home, and sprinted the section through the cemetery. I tore across our front lawn, avoiding Chana's aerial assault.

With my backpack still strapped to my back, I stood in the kitchen heaving ragged breaths.

Zippy's text had been charged with urgency, but she looked calm in her office. She was examining something on the computer, squinting at the screen. "The rabbi called," she said as she typed something. "Two of them actually. Moritz *and* Friedman."

"The graves were—"

"Don't explain yourself. We don't have time. They asked me for Dad's cell."

"So you gave them a fake number, disconnected our landline, incinerated our mailbox, and legally changed our last names to Smith."

"That is not what I did."

My breathing was finally slowing, just as my anxiety was ramping up. I slipped my backpack onto the floor and readjusted my tzitzis. "I think we should deny it outright," I said. "Nip it right in the butt."

"Did you just say nip it in the *butt*?"

"No?"

"It's *bud*. With a—it's a flower—oy, darling brother."

Zippy stopped typing and pivoted in her chair. She crossed her legs at the knees. "Do you know what the Gemara says about lying? 'Truth is the seal of the Holy One, blessed be He.' Rashi says that where there is truth, there is God, and we—"

"Feel his absence whenever falsehoods are told. Duh, bro. Still, I think we should try it."

"Yeah? You do? Okay. I'll humor you. Go ahead. Try it. Pretend I'm Dad."

I cleared my throat. "Why hello, Abba. Welcome home. I trust you had a productive and pleasant day as the primary breadwinner of this family, winning all kinds of delicious bread."

"All right. A bit glib, but a fine start."

"You may have heard some mishegoss from Rabbi Moritz.

But don't listen to him. You see, the rebbe, though he is well-intentioned, is a schizophrenic, and he suffers from hallucinations, each more vivid and outlandish than the next."

Zippy put up a hand. "I'm going to stop you there. Now, do you see, brother, how the lie you've told is both (a) implausible, and (b) offensive to those with a serious mental illness?"

"Do we have string cheese?"

"Focus."

"Fine. Fine. Okay. What do you suggest?"

"Plead the Fifth. Eat string cheese. Say nothing. Let me speak for you. Look contrite, obsequious."

"I'm going to need a dictionary to pull that off."

Zippy chortled. She didn't want to but couldn't help it. "Why are you clever in all the wrong ways? Look like you're sorry."

"I didn't do anything wrong. I did the *right* thing. We're talking about the desecration of *Jewish* graves, an offense to—"

"What do we need to do? Muzzle you? Look. Maybe you don't really understand what you've done. Maybe you don't see how bad this can get. Maybe you're just not that bright. But I'm telling you how to get the best possible outcome. Take it or leave it."

Zippy turned back to the computer. I turned to the fridge and went to find my string cheese muzzle.

As I extracted the pack of string cheese, the front door opened.

"Stand close to me," Zippy whispered, "so I can give you nonverbal cues." She pulled me toward her, gripping the bottom of my shirt with her fist, like a puppeteer taking control of a puppet.

It should be said that my father is a mild-mannered person. He is generally thoughtful and calm. When you shake his hand, he grips yours just the right way, like his hand is embracing yours rather than squeezing it.

He is named for Abraham, and the day before my bar mitzvah he said this to me: "I do my best to serve HaShem. But if I'd been Abraham, I don't know if I could have made the covenant with God. I could have bound my son and brought him up the mountain. This I could have done. But I don't think I could have gone through with the sacrifice." He hung his head in shame when he said this, though, personally, I felt pretty good about him not wanting to sacrifice me.

"He was trying to tell you that he loves you," Zippy explained later.

"Because he's not willing to slit my throat in a ritual ceremony?"

"Yeah. He was telling you that you make him weak, that the love for his son is the only thing that could keep him from serving his God."

I say that so that I can contrast it with this: When my father burst through the front door, he looked ready to bind and sacrifice everyone in sight. He did not look tender. He looked like he was going to tenderize me like a piece of meat.

He flew into the kitchen, his face red, his mouth Moritzesque in its moisture: spitting venom like a snake. I held the pack of string cheese out in front of me like a shield.

"How could you?" he growled. "How *could* you? *My* son. I—I don't have words."

This is what people say when they have a lot of words.

I did as Zippy had instructed me. I didn't even look at my dad. I pulled a plastic-encased string cheese away from its brethren, watched it separate itself along the perforated edge. I picked at the top flap of the string cheese, and peeled it open.

Zippy too kept her eyes down. She looked at her computer keyboard, but spoke to my father. "He's sorry. He didn't understand what he was doing. He was trying to do the right thing."

"Betraying your community is the right thing? Betraying your family is the right thing? Betraying your father is the right thing?"

Instinctively, I opened my mouth to answer, but Zippy pinched me in the back and I snapped my mouth shut.

Zippy spoke slowly, calmly. "He's sorry. He just didn't understand."

I wasn't sorry at all, but I kept my mouth clamped shut. I peeled off thin strands of gossamer cheese with a practiced motion. I tried to pretend that the world contained only me and cheese, which, frankly, is how the world *should* be.

Zippy was trying to get my dad to direct his attention to her, but I could feel him looking at me now. His eyes were hot. "You got a picture, right? Before you erased the graffiti, you got a picture, correct?"

I looked at Zippy.

She closed her eyes and exhaled in resignation. She'd forgotten to ask me if I'd taken a picture. She did not know. She was a poor lawyer. I would have to answer for myself. I was on my own.

"Why would I take a picture?" I asked.

"What he meant to say—" Zippy began.

"Why? he asks, like an am ha'aretz, like a complete fool. Why should he take a picture? For proof, that's why. For proof he should take a picture."

"I was righting a *clear* wrong. What I did was a mitzvah." How no one else could see that I'd done a good deed was beyond me.

"He thinks he was doing a mitzvah," my father reflected, talking to himself, or to God. "He thinks it was a *mitzvah*." Then he turned back to me. "At least if you'd left them there, at least if you had a photo, we would have *one* good thing, one thing to hang our hats on."

"I don't get—" I started. "You *want* them to hate us? You want people to see . . . how could it be—"

"We could *show* them, show them what happens when they spread their hate, show them what their blind bigotry has done. With this, we'd have leverage. With this, we could have scared them into changing the law. With this, we could be building by next week. Then we could say to the community, to the congregation, 'Well, yes, it doesn't look good, but really Yehuda has helped us out. He has helped our cause. He has joined in our fight to make a little place for ourselves here. It looks bad, yes, but he is helping.' But now? Now he's embarrassed me. How can this be *my* son? He's betrayed me, and we have nothing to show for it. It was for *nothing*."

The last "nothing" came out in a growl. My father was breathing fairly heavily now, his face flushed. He had a quiet,

simmering rage I'd never seen before. He didn't usually talk about me like I wasn't there. And he'd never looked at me like this, like he didn't know me, like he didn't *want* to know me.

I felt trapped, claustrophobic, like an animal in a too-small cage. We were all in this little space, a kind of bottleneck where the hall met the kitchen.

Now two more people joined us. Hearing their approach, my father glanced behind him, and his face softened a bit when he saw Rivkie and Goldie. He still wanted to know *them*. They looked scared. Rivkie's little eyes darted around, first at Dad, then at Zippy, finally at me.

They were little girls, all innocence.

My father turned around and scooped them both up. He spun back to face me, one sister in each arm. He was pointing them at me, like weapons.

Rivkie and Goldie both stared at me. Their little faces, pudgy still with baby fat, faced mine, and they silently begged me to stop, to end the argument.

It was unfair what he was doing, using them like this. Their wide eyes were fearful, and I wanted to make it stop, to make their eyes go back to normal, to calm the house down so they could go back upstairs and terrorize each other in peace.

And I would have done that if my father hadn't said, "How could you do this to me?"

I didn't do anything to *him*. If I'd done anything wrong—which I hadn't—I thought he would care about me looking away from Torah. I thought his anger would be about how I

couldn't serve God if my thoughts were focused on the gentile world, or a gentile girl. But he only cared about how my actions reflected on him. He cared about how it would make him look in front of the community. He should have been proud of me. But he only cared about his political battle, how the grave desecrations could help him get his precious apartment building off the ground.

"I have a lesson for all of you," my father said. "Listen."

When he said "all of you" he meant me exclusively, but Rivkie and Goldie looked up at him from their seats in his arms, and Zippy looked up politely from the table.

I looked down at my cheese, trying to make thinner and thinner strips, but Zippy prodded me with her elbow, imploring me to meet my dad's gaze.

I complied.

"Back in the old country," my father began, shifting his weight a little to give Goldie some extra support, "the economy was disastrous, partly because there were no proper banks, because the goyim could not lend money to each other. Their bible told them they were not allowed to charge interest. So they asked the Jews if they would lend money and help everybody prosper. So the Jews did. They made loans available for everybody. They charged fair interest. They turned whole economies around. But then, whenever there were problems, the goyim turned on the Jews. They accused us of being greedy. They blamed the Jews for their poverty. They said everything would be fine if it weren't for the dirty Jewish moneylenders.

They killed the Jews for it, for fairly doing the very thing they had asked of us."

"That's not very nice," Goldie observed.

"No, Goldie. It's *not* very nice. And yet your brother wants to make one of them his girlfriend."

I burned with anger. I hated him using Goldie like this. I didn't like him telling her a violent story like that. "So," I said. "What you're saying is that because I cleaned swastikas off Jewish graves and a girl decided to help me, I'm going to impoverish her and then she'll kill me? No. You're—"

"Hoodie," Zippy said, and I could feel her tugging on the back of my shirt.

But I went on. "Can you explain better how the elaborate analogy pertains to the current situation? Are you actually worried about me? Or is it just about you? Is it just about them taking down your money operation?"

"Hoodie," said Goldie.

"Yehuda," my dad said—everybody was just saying my name now in different variations. My dad put the girls down, first Rivkie, then Goldie. He readjusted his suit jacket.

Zippy saw it coming. There was something menacing and violent coming, and Zippy saw it. "Yehuda will go to his room," she said.

"Yehuda, *you*—" my father began.

"Yehuda will go to his room," Zippy repeated. Then she said it again, quiet but firm. She said it over and over again, rhythmically, like a drumbeat. I marched to that beat. I didn't want to. But it was the only way. I marched past Rivkie and Goldie, dodged Leah on the stairs, and only stopped marching when my bedroom door closed behind me.

My room is the smallest in the house—it's only about one and a half times the size of my body—but still it's mine, and mine alone.

It's a different experience for my friends, like Moshe Tzvi, who have brothers. Nobody farts on me in my sleep, or fills my sleep mittens with peanut butter. Chana did put mayonnaise in my shoes one time, but that was on me. If you don't lock your door, you better double-check your shoes for mayo before you put them on. And anyway, it wasn't as uncomfortable as you'd imagine. I think if you're going to have a footwear condiment, mayo is the way to go. It has an almost orthotic viscosity, and it doesn't stain like mustard or ketchup.

Having my own room is the only advantage of being the only boy in the family, but it's a big advantage.

For example, after my dad quiet-yelled at me about the graffiti and Anna-Marie, I was able to retreat to my own space, and wallow in misery all by myself. And because I have my own room, I'm the only person in the world who knows if I cried or not—I didn't.

Fun fact about me: I've actually never cried before. I'm stoic and void of emotion, like one of those monoliths: imposing, stalwart, unfeeling.

When I'm upset, I start by trying to talk to God. The

problem with talking to him is that the answers he provides aren't always easy to decipher. So then I turn to Zippy or Moshe Tzvi, who, of the people I know, are the best at interpreting God's teachings and messages.

When I was done not crying, I was about to walk back downstairs to talk to Zippy, but I wasn't sure the coast was clear. So I was going to pick up my phone and call Moshe Tzvi, but I realized that I didn't want to talk to him about this. He wouldn't understand. In order to get what I was going through, he'd have to experience normal human feelings, like empathy.

The person I wanted to talk to was Anna-Marie. She was empathetic. She had an understanding smile. She didn't condescend. If she were here, she could put her hand on my arm and reassure me. Because she'd been there with me, and it was so clear to both of us that what we'd done had been the right thing.

I stared up at my ceiling, picturing her face among the cracks in the plaster. Was she going through the same thing? Had her mother chewed her out for hanging out with the wrong person, going on a date with the enemy? Was my new friend—my new *girl*friend—staring at her ceiling, not teary-eyed, wondering how I was doing, wishing I was there so we could deal with it together, like we'd dealt with the graffiti?

When it came time to sleep, I couldn't. It had been a long day. I was exhausted. I covered my eyes with my hand, said the Shema prayer, and lay there expectantly. But sleep would not come.

Eventually I got up and padded downstairs to the kitchen, because that's where the cheese sleeps. Zippy too. I only noticed her when I opened the fridge and the fridge light illuminated the room. She was asleep in the wooden kitchen chair, her head thrown back, her mouth open. She was making a quiet whistling sound, harmonizing with the buzz of the fridge. The fingers of her right hand were still wrapped around the handle of her coffee mug, and her left hand was draped over the laptop keyboard.

I selected cheeses from drawers and brought them to the table.

I was still thinking about Anna-Marie. I understood why the rabbis didn't want me to have these thoughts. They were Pringles-esque: Once you started, you could not stop. It was like an addiction. You know it's bad when even cheese won't take your mind off of it.

The unkosher thoughts made me reach for the computer. I pulled it carefully out from under Zippy's fingers. She picked the hand up and used it to scratch herself near her ear, but she remained asleep.

We didn't have Wi-Fi until last year. "What good will come of Wi-Fi?" my father had said. "All our years we've never had Wi-Fi. Why now should we have Wi-Fi? It is a passageway to a sick world, Wi-Fi. I will not sit by and watch that sickness infect my children."

But Zippy said she needed internet for college.

"Then perhaps you've chosen the wrong college," Dad replied.

Zippy explained, in her respectful Zippy way, that if we did not get Wi-Fi, she would have to move out.

The next day my father walked into the house with a brand-new laptop and a guy from the cable company.

I reached for the laptop now, woke it up, and prepared to be infected. I brought up the internet browser and punched a few keys. I had my desired results immediately. I thanked God for giving Anna-Marie a distinctive and uncommon name.

The first thing that came up was Instagram, but I couldn't actually see Anna-Marie's pictures. They were hidden because I didn't "follow" her.

The next thing was a video app called TikTok. Her videos were not hidden. When I clicked the videos, she was right there, in my kitchen.

In the first video I clicked, her face was right in front of the camera. She was looking straight into my eyes. She was smiling at me. I knew she couldn't see me, but I smiled back at her. She was saying the words to a song, her lips moving in sync with the person rapping the lyrics. As the video wrapped up, she laughed to herself and produced a shy, embarrassed look. With a flip of her hair she turned off the camera, like she suddenly felt uncomfortable making eye contact with me. When the video ended, it simply began again. I watched it a whole bunch of times—let's not speculate about the exact number.

The second video was shot from a wider angle. Anna-Marie stood in the middle of a neat bedroom with a green color scheme. It had to be her room. Through the computer screen, she was letting me into *her* bedroom.

She wore sweatpants with vertical lettering on the legs, and a T-shirt that ended just above the pants. Her hair was wet like she'd just gotten out of the shower. She began the video by saying something. I had to restart it to hear: "This is for the Tree-11 girls." Then a song started, and Anna-Marie began a dance. The dance had a lot of complicated arm motions. She sent her long arms out one way, then the other, then bent them behind her head, then put them on her hips. Then she started moving her hips.

I slammed the laptop shut. It made a snap that reverberated around the kitchen.

Zippy stirred, squinted. "Hoodie?" she asked.

I said nothing, hoping that she was motion-activated and wouldn't see me if I stayed still. After a long moment, she shifted a little in her chair and began to snore again.

I slowly opened the computer again. I shouldn't have. The dancing gave me a whole bunch of uncomfortable and unsanctioned thoughts.

I knew I shouldn't watch the video again. I knew my dad was right about the sickness you could find on the internet. A good Jewish boy wouldn't watch a video like that.

But then why was my hand opening the screen? Why was I reloading the page, pressing the play button again on the video? Why did I then watch it innumerable times, until I fell asleep at the table?

I woke up with Zippy kicking my chair. "Hoodie. Hoodie. Ye*hu*da. Get upstairs so I can wake you up."

I looked back and forth between her and the laptop, the latter of which was still open on the table in front of me. "Why is your computer staring at me? These things really do have minds of their—"

Zippy shut me up with a snap of her fingers and pointed upstairs, where there were already sounds of parental stirring.

I tiptoed up the stairs and closed my door just in time. Zippy "woke me up" a few minutes later with the traditional door kick.

CHAPTER 5

presented by Starburst, in which Moshe Tzvi and I help a friend in need

THIS SECTION IS BROUGHT TO you by Starburst, the official soft taffy candy of the Moskovitz Torah Academy. However, I'm contractually obligated to say that we have no official affiliation with the Wrigley Company that produces Starbursts, or with Mars, Incorporated, of which the Wrigley Company is a wholly owned subsidiary. Though, to be clear, we're open to such an arrangement—our legal representatives can be reached at [redacted]—as we feel that a synergistic partnership could be beneficial to both parties.

We, the students of the Moskovitz Academy, like Starburst is what I'm saying. They're delicious, and they stick in your teeth, which allows you to enjoy them for a longer period of time. Like, you can eat one, and then thirty minutes later, when you've totally forgotten that you ate one thirty minutes ago, you discover a little morsel lodged in between two molars, and it's the most pleasant of surprises.

The great people at Starburst had just made a "mystery" pack. Both the wrappers and the taffies themselves were an off-white color, and the wrappers were dotted with little question marks. Some of these flavors were delicious and tasted like fruit. Some of them were disgusting, and did not taste like fruit. Moshe Tzvi claimed he once had one that "tasted like dog urine," though he backtracked when we asked him how exactly he knew what dog urine tasted like.

The rebbe was lecturing us and pacing back and forth in front of the board. "What happens when an egg falls off of a roof?" he asked.

"It breaks?" Reuven suggested.

"No, that's—"

"No, Rebbe," I explained, "it *does* break. My sister Chana carried out this very experiment on me just the other day. I *assure* you that the egg breaks."

"Fragility is one of the defining characteristics of the egg," Reuven added. "It's what it's famous for."

"All right. All right," Moritz said. "*Suppose* the egg doesn't break."

"But it *will*," said Ephraim.

Moritz stopped pacing and placed his hands on the desk, facing us. "It's a *symbolic* egg," he said. Moritz was always pressing us to take the moral and ethical teachings of Jewish philosophy less literally. In order to drink of the well that is the Talmud's deep wisdom, you needed to see its lessons as just that: lessons. The world has changed since the Talmud was first written, but what's amazing about the Talmud is that its teachings apply to today just as they applied to biblical times, just as they will apply to the lives of the sentient robot Jews a thousand years from now.

The lesson he was trying to teach us was about property and the relationships between good neighbors. The main question was this: If an egg rolls off your roof, then down a hill into your neighbor's yard, to whom does the egg belong? Is it still your egg, because it was laid by your chicken? Or does it now belong to your neighbor because it resides on their property?

But we were having trouble getting past the practical details.

"Why would you go through the trouble of bringing a single egg up on the roof?" Moshe Tzvi asked. "Perhaps we should be more focused on the mental health of the person who's done that." Our star student was participating less than usual, because he was otherwise occupied. Moshe Tzvi had a pack of mystery Starburst in front of him on his desk. He was opening each Starburst one by one and taking a tiny bite off the corner. If he liked it, he ate it. If he didn't like it, he fed it to Chaim Abramowitz.

By the way, I was now the best shooter on the JV basketball team, at least for the time being. Chaim couldn't shoot at all for the foreseeable future, because he'd broken both of his arms. Well, the stone wall at the side of the school had broken both of his arms. Or Aharon Bernstein, who'd introduced Chaim to the wall, had broken both of his arms. As in a Gemara passage, the assignment of responsibility was the subject of heated debate, and depended on your perspective.

Either way, both of his arms were broken, in a total of nineteen places. Chaim claimed that this was a record: "Dr. Reznikov says he's never seen that many fractures in both arms at the same time. He says they shattered, and I quote, 'like panes of cheap glass.' He says he might write up a journal article about my left one, because he thinks the shattering is unpreced—"

"Nobody likes a braggart, Chaim."

Our egg-possession lesson was punctuated here and there by Chaim's flavor announcements. "Sour cherry," he would say. "Vanilla. No. No. Vanilla *bean*."

Moritz went on a brief rant about the necessity of engaging with both holy text and our three-thousand-year-old tradition. Then he put his book down on the desk and stared at us to see if his rant had had the desired effect.

Chaim broke the silence. "This one is lychee."

"Is it?" Moshe Tzvi replied. "Go ahead and tell us what lychee is, then."

"It's this flavor," said Chaim, with a grin.

Moshe Tzvi did not appreciate Chaim's back talk, and he stuffed a new Starburst right through Chaim's grin.

Chaim's expression changed immediately. First it was a grimace, then a more intense grimace. Then, suddenly, he was gagging, violent gags that bordered on retches. When he finally found his voice, he produced a single word: "Cinnamon."

"Cinnamon is delicious," I said.

"No. No. Taffy should *not* be cinnamon. Oh my goodness. Rebbe. Rebbe. Can I go wash my mouth?"

The rebbe had resigned himself and he was looking out the windows behind us and scratching at his beard. Now he lowered his gaze and eyed Chaim. "Can you?" he asked. "How exactly are you going to manage that?"

Chaim looked at his hands, bound in casts from shoulders to fingers, bent ninety degrees at the elbows, and he despaired, "Oh no. No. No."

"Can we have a volunteer to help Chaim wash his mouth out?" the rebbe asked the room.

Everybody raised his hand immediately. We cared deeply about our dear friend Chaim. We all wanted to be there for him in his time of need.

Chaim looked at each of us in turn. The fear in his eyes was palpable. He started to whimper. "Why? What have I done to deserve this? The egg, Rebbe. Whose is it? What does Rashi say about the egg? Please, tell me."

But Rabbi Moritz had decided to make an example of Chaim.

Moshe Tzvi and I stationed ourselves on either side of Chaim. We each took one of his arms, stood him up, and led him out of the classroom.

In the hall, we looked at each other across Chaim. "Now, cinnamon is one of the stronger flavors out there," said Moshe Tzvi. "Stronger even, some say, than lychee."

"They do say that," I agreed. "It is likely we'll have to take extreme measures to eradicate such a flavor from the tender taste buds of young Mr. Abramowitz."

"Under ordinary circumstances, I would think that a few Tic Tacs would do the trick."

"But just look at Chaim," I said. "Behold the level of oral discomfort he's experiencing."

"Agreed. That's a most perspicacious observation, Hoodie. These circumstances are indeed extraordinary. I fear we will have to pull out all of the proverbial stops."

"Guys," Chaim said as we led him down the hall. "I'm right here. I can still talk. I broke my *arms*. Tic Tacs are fine."

"Sha, sha, Chaim," said Moshe Tzvi. "Don't get excited. Remain calm. We'll get through this together."

Chaim did get excited. He sustained a high level of excitement all the way through the operation. He called us names, fought us through the bathroom door, then struggled to get his head out from under the soap dispenser.

"It foams automatically," Moshe Tzvi told him soothingly. "It's gentle."

But Chaim did not listen to Moshe Tzvi's advice, and continued to toss his face around, flapping his head up and down like a fish on land. He ended up with the gentle foam in his eyes, which caused him to produce a series of gentle whimpers.

Once we got his mouth open, he gave up the fight, and let us go through with the cleansing process. When it was over, and he was doubled over the sink coughing and heaving, Moshe Tzvi said, "See? That wasn't so bad, was it?"

"No," Chaim managed, attempting to speak, "It was hor—hor . . . it was hor . . ."

"What word is he trying to say?" I asked Moshe Tzvi. "I can't think of any words that begin that way. I assume he's trying to thank us."

"Almost assuredly," said Moshe Tzvi. "It's okay, Chaim. You don't have to thank us. You would have done the same for us."

Chaim was now attempting to rinse the final suds from his mouth, but the only way he could activate the sink was with a wave of his hand. The issue was that by the time Chaim got his mouth down to the faucet, it turned off.

Moshe Tzvi and I leaned against the wall and watched him work. We offered to help, but he told us that we'd "helped enough."

Chaim had thrown his kippah off his head, and Moshe Tzvi reached down to replace it.

I went back to the videos of Anna-Marie, the ones I'd been replaying in my head all morning. I kept trying to put them out of my mind, but something kept pulling them back in. It was like trying to feed Chana back when she was a baby. You'd put a slice of apple on her high chair, and she would knock it down to the floor, and giggle. And then you'd put the apple slice back up on the little high chair table, and she'd knock it right back off, until you were left with a choice: force it into her like soap into Chaim Abramowitz, or give up and let her win.

If I kept trying to put Anna-Marie out of my head, and she kept returning, was she *supposed* to be there? And anyway, what harm was it doing?

When she popped into my head in the bathroom, I instinctively looked at my tzitzis down by my hips. The hanging tassels were supposed to remind me of the mitzvahs, the commandments. But when I looked at them, they danced back and forth, and made me think about the chain that danced on Anna-Marie's neck, and then Anna-Marie dancing in the video, and then I was back in her bedroom, the place where she danced, and slept, and dressed, and, you know, undressed.

When I shut the computer last night, did I do it because it was wrong of her to be so immodest? Or was it because I'd just been *told* that it was wrong to look at something like that?

I've always done what I'm told. Well, no, that's not even remotely true. What I mean is that I always questioned the little things. But I never really questioned the big picture: pass my yeshiva classes and graduate, go to a post–high school program and study more, marry an Orthodox girl, go to college or rabbinical school. Take the well-worn path, you know? The worn path doesn't have any brambles or, like, bramble-adjacent plants in your way. But with Anna-Marie dancing around in front of my mind's eye, the path I was on didn't feel so hazard-free.

"Do you ever wonder if it's all too much?" I asked Moshe Tzvi.

Moshe Tzvi looked up from Chaim. "You know Chaim would have done the same to us if we'd broken all of *our* arms. He knows it too."

"That's not what I meant. I mean, like, all of this." I waved my arms, indicating the world around me. But this bathroom looked like any other, so I had to clarify. "Being Jewish. Being frum. Following the commandments. Praying three times a day. Saying every blessing. Do you ever feel like it's just too much? Like, you're already wearing a lot of clothes, and then people just keep draping jackets and coats, and more jackets and coats over you, until you can barely stand, and you're doubled over under all that material. And then they tell you to stand up straighter, that it's disrespectful to bend, so you try to stand up straighter, but you just can't, because the stuff is too heavy. So you're stuck. You either have to throw off all the layers, or you have to collapse under their weight. And then, while you're already overdressed, you have to walk this trail, but it's overgrown, and you need to use a machete, or even a small but controlled brush fire to clear the path you're on?"

Moshe Tzvi came closer to me. He reached out and rapped on my skull like you'd knock on a door. "Is the real Hoodie in there?" he asked. "Hello?"

I said nothing.

Moshe Tzvi was quiet for a moment. He tapped his foot on the tile floor. "Is it true what they're saying?" he asked. "Is that why Rabbi Moritz seltzered you? You're a traitor now? You're going apikores on us?"

I needed Moshe Tzvi just then. I needed him to stop acting like himself and talk to me seriously. "No. I mean it. Be honest with me. *Do* you? Do you ever question? Do you ever wonder what it's all for?"

He was quiet for a minute. If I didn't know him better, I'd say he was being introspective. We listened to the faucet turn on and off.

"Well," he said. "First, I would turn to Maimonides, whose thirteen principles of faith tell us that one who does not believe, one who does not obey the commandments will find himself among the heretics and the apikorsim, and will perish, while those who do follow will find eternal life. But then I would think about Ibn Ezra, who contradicted Maimonides, and took a much more lenient view, though I suppose his commentary centered on those who questioned the Mosaic *origins* of—"

"I'm not asking Rabbi Gutman. I'm asking my friend Moshe Tzvi if he, personally, ever gets tired of it all. Come on, dude."

"We are what we are, Hoodie. It's like when Menachem Meiri, in the twelfth century—"

"No, *bad* Moshe Tzvi."

"Okay. Okay. It's like, Christians have to be Christians. Hindus have to be Hindus. We all have to live *some* way. We all have to *be* somebody or something. Have I ever wondered if I'm the thing I'm supposed to be, or what it would be like to be somebody else? Of course. And yes, it feels like a lot. It *is* a lot. God asks a lot of us. But think about the alternative. Aren't you *thankful* to be a Jew? I am. My life has more *meaning* because of it. God's Torah was given to *me*, to *my* people. It's a privilege. Dude, think about that feeling you get on Simchas Torah, when you dance with God's Torah in your hands, when you celebrate with all of your people, with every Jew, holding God's words to Moses on Sinai in your hands. There is no burden I wouldn't take on in exchange for that feeling."

"Just make the kid a rabbi now," Chaim said, looking at

his immobilized hands, perhaps imagining them holding the Torah. "Great sermon, Rebbe."

"Plus," Moshe Tzvi said, "tonight is Shabbos. Think about *Shabbos*, Hoodie, and all of the food, and also the . . . food. And just, like, all of the other great stuff, like the . . . food."

I like Simchas Torah. Solid holiday. Top ten for sure. But when I'm dancing with the Torah, I'm never thinking about God or Moses or Sinai. I'm mostly trying not to drop the Torah. And the Torah isn't the part that makes me happy. What makes me happy is that everybody around me is happy, that I can see joy on the faces of my family, and my friends. I'm not thinking about God or Moses. I'm thinking about the Jews I *know*. Maybe I'm doing it wrong. It's the same thing with Shabbos. I like Shabbos because my whole family is forced to be together.

"Hoodie?" Moshe Tzvi asked. "You still with us?"

"Mostly," I said.

Rabbi Moritz popped his head into the bathroom. "Come," he said. "Let's go back to class."

"Great idea, Rebbe," Moshe Tzvi said. "We got preoccupied talking about the egg. There's just *so* much to say. It's overwhelming. I can't speak for misters Rosen or Abramowitz, but I personally feel overwhelmed by it."

Moritz straightened his suit. I guess he couldn't tell if Moshe Tzvit was patronizing him, or seriously engaging. The answer was both, but Moritz always felt it had to be one or the other.

CHAPTER 6

in which I have forbidden thoughts about slow-cooked chicken

WE GET OUT OF SCHOOL early on Fridays for the Sabbath.

When I got home, my mom and Zippy were preparing the house for Shabbos: cleaning, cooking, setting the table in the dining room. They were dressed up already. Zippy's dark curls shone from her shower. My mom was wearing her sheitel instead of her usual headscarf. She looked like a completely different person, more elegant. The wig was straight and brunette, and made her look older and more distinguished, like a founding father. That probably wasn't the look she was going for. Most moms aren't trying to look like Thomas Jefferson, but I thought it suited her in a weird way.

It was always odd to see my mother in the kitchen. It was odd to see her at all these days. When Zippy and I got old enough to watch the little girls, my mom went back to work. And it was like she had to make up for lost time: In the mornings, Mom taught at the girls' school that Chana and Leah attended, then worked at another school in the afternoon, before spending her evenings teaching other women how to teach. She spent most of her home time in her office nook in the bedroom. At this point, she was like a bat who only emerged from her cave on Fridays, when she and Zippy prepared the house for the Sabbath. But that's why Shabbos was Shabbos, so we could put down our work and all be together.

"Why are you smiling at us like a creep?" Zippy asked me.

"Who's smiling? I'm not smiling. *You're* smiling," I said. "Man, that smell."

"It's the Crock-Pot," my mom said. "Pulled chicken. Barbeque. Don't even *think* about touching it."

But I was already thinking about it. This was a banner day for me thinking about things I wasn't supposed to think about.

It's hard to beat the smells of Friday afternoon. You can't cook on Shabbos, so you have to make everything beforehand. Or you have to get it in the Crock-Pot beforehand. You can leave the Crock-Pot on, so long as you started it already.

I let out a deep breath I didn't realize I'd been holding. I closed my eyes, leaned on the doorjamb, and just let all the aromas wash over me.

"You can thank us by making sure all of the lights are out," Zippy said to me. "But leave the living room lights on. Ma, are you thinking we should leave the fan on?"

"Your call. You're going to have to make these decisions soon for you and Yoel."

"Leave the ceiling fan on," Zippy told me. "I checked with Rabbi Google, and he says it's going to be hot this weekend."

Until pretty recently, we didn't have to prepare as meticulously. While Rivkie was still a baby, if we wanted to turn on a light, we could hold her up near the light switch. Eventually, out of sheer curiosity, she would flip it.

The trick was that if she didn't know what she was actually *doing* when she flipped the switch, it didn't violate Shabbos. In theory, we could even watch TV, so long as we were okay with whatever channel happened to pop on when Rivkie tripped on the remote. But now Rivkie knew what a light switch was, and she was a remote control expert. So unless another baby comes along, we have to prepare more carefully, because once a switch is flipped, it stays flipped. If we mess up and leave the home shopping channel on at full volume, they will shout sales at us until there are three stars in the sky on Saturday night.

We all gathered in the dining room twenty minutes before sundown. We looked our best. I had on my best suit and my Borsalino. I matched my father almost perfectly. I was wearing the literal coats and jackets, but they didn't feel too heavy. I stood up straight.

We stood there for a minute while Zippy untucked Rivkie's skirt, then we welcomed Shabbos and my mom lit the candles. There was a pleasant warmth in the room.

The good warmth evaporated when we got outside. It was only me, my dad, and Zippy, and it didn't feel right.

Back in Colwyn there was an eruv, a piece of twine wrapped

around the town. Within the eruv, you could push strollers and carry children, things that were otherwise forbidden on Shabbos.

Here in Tregaron there was no eruv, at least not yet. The mayor and her council wouldn't allow it. The synagogue was too far for Rivkie to walk, so we left the younger girls behind with Mom, and headed out with our skeleton crew.

But it wasn't the same, and I missed our old Friday night walks to shul. We would meet up with other families on the way to the synagogue, and I would walk with a big group of my friends, and our sisters would create flash mobs of girls running around, just a sea of little skirts twirling about.

Families would call greetings to each other from across the street, or even walk in the street, since nobody was driving anywhere. It was like a little festival. After a week of hard work, we all got together to celebrate our rest.

But in Tregaron it was different, and it was getting worse.

We walked in silence. Zippy's shoes clopped on the sidewalk. When we got closer to town, we ran into other community families. But we didn't call to them. Nobody felt comfortable drawing attention to themselves.

When we ran into the Gutmans, they just fell in line with us. We didn't even murmur greetings.

I could almost see why the town thought of us as an invasion. In a lot of ways, we looked like an army. We were dressed in uniform, marching on the town.

"We stick out like sore thumbs," I whispered to Moshe Tzvi.

"*Do* sore thumbs stick out?" he asked. "Do you ever see

a pair of thumbs and think, 'Man, those thumbs are *sore*'?"

There were a lot of non-Jews out. They were all back from their summer vacations, walking, riding bicycles, driving. I'd never looked up and paid attention to the gentiles when I walked to shul, even in Tregaron. But now I did. As they rode by, they eyed us suspiciously, gave us these quick glances, ones that were designed not to be seen. But they were obvious. I felt each of them.

The opposite happened on the sidewalk. As we got to the busy business district of town, we would literally run into groups of goyim. But instead of shooting us furtive and disapproving glances, they acted like we weren't there, like we were invisible. If we didn't move out of the way, they would walk into us. When there was a group of gentiles coming the other way on the sidewalk, we had to dodge into the street.

Moshe Tzvi and I almost got hit by an SUV. It stopped inches from us and honked. When the woman behind the wheel was done leaning on the horn, she threw her hands up in the air. I tried to indicate the busy sidewalk, to show her that we didn't have any room there. She rolled her eyes at me. Only Mr. Gutman's hand on his arm stopped Moshe Tzvi from giving her the finger.

Right before we got to the synagogue door, my father bumped into an older woman. "I'm sorry," he said. "My apologies."

"*Excuse* me," she said. She had dyed red hair, and beady green eyes. She stared at my father in disgust. "E*xcuse* me," she repeated. "Do you *ever* look where you're going?"

"Me personally?" my father asked. He remained his usual restrained self. He looked respectable, standing tall. He held his arms loose in front of him, crossed slightly at the wrist: a pose of calm.

The woman was not calm, and her eyes darted around at each of us, never resting. She huffed audibly.

"Or are you referring to *all* of us?" my dad asked. "Are we not allowed to walk to our place of worship?"

"Avraham, let's just go inside," Mr. Gutman said to him.

"Excuse me," the woman repeated, and she pushed her way by my dad.

Inside, I instinctively started to feel better—a synagogue is a safe place. But then my dad gave me this new look. It was a "told you so" kind of look. His eyes said: See? They'll hit you with their cars. They'll yell at you on the sidewalk. And this is only the beginning. You think it's okay to hang out with these people?

These people? The ones who pushed him on the street? No. I didn't think that lady and I would have gotten along. But if we tossed Anna-Marie in with her, how was that different from the way they were treating us, like we were all one collective being? But I couldn't say any of that, because he hadn't actually asked.

My father wasn't the only person looking at me askance.

We split before we went in for the service. Zippy headed around the corner toward the women's section, and I went directly into the sanctuary with my dad, the Gutman men, and Zippy's fiancé, Yoel.

The congregation had been much bigger back in Colwyn.

Our sanctuary there was big and open. There were wooden benches with blue cushions and silver chandeliers hanging from the high ceiling. It had an almost regal aura to it, and you could feel the presence of God there.

Here in Tregaron, we sat on folding chairs—there were real chairs on order, supposedly. Before we leased it, the building had been a pool supply store—there were pool noodles on the floor the first time we prayed. The ceiling was low, the room cramped. I couldn't feel God in there.

As I sat down, I could feel eyes on me. I couldn't catch people actually staring, but still I knew they were watching.

I should have known. In a small community, the grapevine is high-speed. So if a rabbi sees you in a cemetery with the antisemitic mayor's daughter, by the next day the whole community knows about it, and they're giving you quick, sharp looks of disapproval. Their heads are in their prayer books, and they're bowing and chanting before God. But you know they're thinking about you, looking at you, taking a moment of their Shabbos to disapprove of you.

When the service started, I tried to get lost in it. But I couldn't. I was stuck in my own head, feeling each minute pass slowly. Usually, I felt as one with the men around me, all of us together communing with God. But that night I felt separate, like I was in my own section of the synagogue, praying alone.

When the service was over, we mingled in the lobby and out on the street in front of the temple. "Good Shabbos," we said, "good Shabbos."

Everybody said "good Shabbos" to me, but that was all they said. Usually they would linger and talk to me, but not tonight. When people saw me, they just murmured "good Shabbos," and moved on as quickly as possible.

Except for Mr. Gutman. Mr. Gutman is a serious man. The whole Gutman family is quiet, dour, serious. It makes you think Moshe Tzvi was adopted, but he just looks too much like them. They all have these icy blue eyes that make you feel cold when you look at them.

Before the walk home, Mr. Gutman came up and stood there. He didn't look at me. He looked out at the street, at the cars passing by, at the store awnings on the opposite curb. "Your father is a good man," he told the street. "Treat him as he deserves to be treated. Treat him as a Jewish son treats his father."

Whenever anybody reprimands me, sarcasm is my go-to response. Sarcasm is a versatile tool, like one of those knives that's also a screwdriver. You can use it with your friends, with your parents, with your teachers. The only place you *can't* use it is with somebody else's dad. It's just . . . not allowed. So I said nothing and waited patiently for Mr. Gutman to walk away. I watched the SUVs speed by, figuring that if he lingered for too long, I could always end the conversation by tossing myself in front of one of them.

Just as I was eyeing a nice new blue Explorer, Moshe Tzvi arrived, and he and I split off from our families. We met up with Ephraim and Shlomo Reznikov, and the four of us trailed behind the main group, walking up the slope of the business strip toward the residential neighborhood.

Moshe Tzvi was saying something about the way the rabbi had led the service—he had a strong opinion about it. But nobody was listening to him. Ephraim and Shlomo were talking about the upcoming Eagles season, wondering if they had enough offensive line depth to protect the quarterback in the event of an injury. Shlomo twirled his right side curl in his finger as he walked, nodding along with his brother's point about the Eagles' new swing tackle.

I wasn't paying attention to either conversation, so I was the one who noticed them.

A group of kids about our age had just popped out of the ice-cream shop. They were strolling lazily down the sidewalk, laughing with each other. Every moment or so, each of them would dip a spoon into ice cream, or press something on the device in their hand.

There were three girls and two guys. One of the girls had her arm draped over the first guy's shoulder, and he had his hand on her hip. The second guy looked up just in time to see us. "Whoa," he said. "I forgot it was Friday, when all these werewolves come out and walk our streets."

For some reason, I didn't even register the werewolf part. The part that got me was how he said "our" streets, like he owned them. I even looked down to see if there was something particularly goyishe about the sidewalk.

I could sense Moshe Tzvi opening his mouth next to me. I

tried to kick his foot to stop him from talking—I didn't want him to embarrass us by saying words—but I missed his foot, kicked the goyishe sidewalk, stubbed my toe, and then had to pretend I hadn't just randomly kicked the sidewalk and stubbed my toe.

"Werewolves come out on a full moon, not on a Friday," Moshe Tzvi corrected, setting the record straight on werewolf behavior. "Unless the two coincide, of course."

I noticed that the rest of our crowd had moved on. The four of us were pack animals separated from the herd, vulnerable. I wanted to run, but knew it would look bad if we ran. It looks silly when people just, like, start running for no apparent reason.

This kid was wearing a T-shirt and gym shorts and had a wide grin. "I guess you would know, you and your freak friends," he said to Moshe Tzvi.

"Hoodie's not a werewolf," said a voice.

It was Anna-Marie. She had been hanging back a little bit, but now she stepped forward, next to the talking guy. "Hey, Hoodie," she said. She forced a smile and waved at me with her ice-cream cup hand. "This is Hoodie," she said, indicating me with her spoon. "He's not a werewolf."

I didn't think I'd ever be so pleased to be specifically identified as a non-werewolf, but it was awesome. I couldn't help but smile. She was like our knight in shining armor, riding up from the back of her group to save us from this goyishe dragon.

"How do *you* know?" I asked her. "You've never seen me on a full moon."

Anna-Marie didn't laugh at my excellent joke. She looked uncomfortable. She kept glancing back and forth between the two groups. "Uh," she said. "Hoodie, this is Case." The talking guy was Case. The non-talking guy was Jaden. Because Jaden's one hand was busy touching the top of the girl's butt, the girl had to feed him his ice cream. The feeder was Cassidy. The last one was Tess.

I started to introduce my friends but it didn't go well. It was a strategic error to start with Shlomo.

"He looks normal speed to me," Case said.

Jaden laughed. He started moving his free arm, and then his mouth, in slow motion. He made his voice deep, like a recording slowed down: "Mayyybeeee heeee issss sssslooowww mennntalllyyy. Yoouuuu knnooooww, innnn hiisss braaiiiiinnn."

The brothers Reznikov looked at each other. "We can't be talking to girls like this," Ephraim said, and he and Shlomo speed-walked around Anna-Marie's group, keeping their eyes down. They went as fast as they could without running.

"See?" Case said. "Pretty fast, actually. I don't think I could walk that fast in one of those vampire suits. Maybe they're more like vampires? Except instead of being allergic to the sun, they're allergic to girls. Hey, Cassidy, try touching this one and see if he explodes."

Case laughed at his own joke, then paused to eat some ice cream. "How do you *know* this kid?" he asked Anna-Marie.

"I live right across from their school. I see him when I walk Borneo."

"Let's go," Moshe Tzvi said to me. "These guys are going to

burn in hell. We can let them enjoy their ice cream before their eternal suffering."

I looked past Anna-Marie's group, and realized I could no longer see any of our people. Moshe Tzvi was right.

"Yeah, let us enjoy our ice cream before you guys take over our town and impose sharia law," said Case.

Moshe Tzvi looked at me. His look said: Are we going to correct his misunderstanding of Abrahamic religions? Are we going to take his ice cream and rub it all over his face? Are we going to murder him in cold blood, and *then* rub his ice cream all over his face? When you've been friends basically since your bris, you can communicate a lot through a single look.

I gave him a reply look that said no to all three questions.

"Anna-Marie is my friend," I said. I wasn't sure who I was talking to: Moshe Tzvi? Case? Myself?

Case, Jaden, and Cassidy all laughed like I'd made a joke. Tess and Anna-Marie exchanged a look, the same kind Moshe Tzvi and I had just shared, the kind that says a lot without saying anything. I couldn't decipher it.

Moshe Tzvi grabbed my arm and pulled me around them, dragging me by the sleeve. But I broke free when I saw that Anna-Marie had separated herself from her group and was walking cautiously back toward me. "Just wait *one* sec," I told Moshe Tzvi. "I promise. I'm coming."

I met Anna-Marie on one of those shaky metal hatches that stores have out front of them that go down into the basement directly from the street.

Anna-Marie was totally different from the free and joyful girl I'd watched dancing in her bedroom. She was looking down at the ground. I should have been angry at her—for a knight, she hadn't been much of a dragon-slayer. She'd mostly stood around looking uncomfortable while the dragon roasted us like marshmallows.

I *tried* to be angry at her. I made an honest effort. But I failed. Instead, I found myself wanting to comfort her, to make her feel better. But I didn't know what to say. We each just stood there looking down at the basement hatch, like the right words would suddenly appear on the ground in front of us. I would have reached out and put my hand on her arm, but I knew Moshe Tzvi was watching.

To keep from doing anything stupid, I shoved my hands into my pockets. There were Starburst in there. I took them out.

"Starburst?" I asked.

She looked up. "Okay," she said. "Look, I—"

"Hoodie!" called Moshe Tzvi. "If you take any longer we're going to have to say Havdalah."

"American Starburst aren't kosher," I told Anna-Marie. "But the Abramowitz market imports them from Britain." Careful not to touch her, I dropped a few of them into her hand, and then started up the street. "Share them with your friends. If you stuff enough of them in Case's mouth, maybe he'll shut up."

"Good idea," she said.

I took off after Moshe Tzvi.

We only had a few moments before we caught up with the

rest of the group. Moshe Tzvi put his face right up to mine. I could smell his hot and sour breath. "You being in love with the mayor's daughter is like being in love with . . . Stalin's daughter," he breathed at me.

"Did Stalin even *have* a daughter? You don't hear a lot about—"

"Svetlana. From his second wife. She was born in 1926."

"I'd date her instead, I guess, but she's a little old for me."

"She's been dead for like ten years."

"Exactly."

"It's not funny, Hoodie." Moshe Tzvi looked legitimately troubled. "It's not something to joke or be sarcastic about. I'll—you know what? I know what to do. I'll use my Shabbos Talmud study for you. I think I can help."

His Talmud study resolution had made him feel better. It hadn't done the same for me, but now we were back among our families, and I couldn't respond.

CHAPTER 7

in which nobody plays board games

FOOD WAS THE ONLY THING that could distract me from the Shabbos service with all of its accusing eyes, and from the werewolf situation on the street with its awkwardness and bigotry.

"Which of these lovely ladies should we devour first?" I asked my assembled family. Two of my mom's roast chickens sat on the table between us.

Goldie had a strong opinion. "We should eat Cluckers first," she said.

"I couldn't agree more," I told her. "Now, Goldie, I hate to be so tactless, but I was never properly introduced. Can you kindly indicate which of our friends here is Cluckers?"

"Can we not anthropomorphize our food?" Zippy asked. "It makes me uncomfortable."

This was a tactical error on Zippy's part, because the rest of us derive a lot of pleasure from her discomfort.

"The clucky one," Goldie clarified.

"Oh, okay. The cluckier one is Cluckers. I see now."

Goldie started making a lot of clucking sounds, so Rivkie joined in. I clucked with them, because it seemed like the thing to do. My dad put his head in his hands in a disapproving way. Zippy put her head in her hands in a not disapproving way.

I reached for the cluckier-looking chicken and served some to my mother.

Back in Colwyn, there weren't a lot of gentiles. I was used to the occasional weird look or sideways glance from non-Jews here and there, but it was different to have a kid your age be outwardly antisemitic. I should have felt scared or hurt, probably. But it just felt surreal. I'd replayed it in my head as I walked the final stretch back to my house, but the fresh memory had an unreal quality to it, as though it were a scene from a movie, not an experience from my real life five minutes before.

Instead of being concerned about the way the kids had made fun of us, I was worried about what Anna-Marie thought. The part of the confrontation that stuck in my mind wasn't the part where I was accused of being a vampire. It was the part where Anna-Marie bit her lip and stared at the ground, and I did the same thing, and neither of us knew what to say.

We ate in silence. No, that's not true. We never do anything in silence. We ate in cacophony, with clucking, shouting, and chewing so loud it could make your ears ring. But it was silence-esque, in that it was the kind of pleasant, familiar cacophony you can just let wash over you.

We had peace around our Shabbos table. And after we'd finished eating, my father started singing.

My father has numerous negative qualities, but he has a great singing voice. We always linger at the Shabbos table on Friday nights and sing z'miros, special Shabbos songs.

On Shabbos, you're supposed to connect with HaShem more closely. Rashi says that on the Sabbath, you're supposed to experience the Torah "mouth to mouth," like you're getting CPR from God. There's an extra soul that comes to you on the Sabbath and connects you to God and his Torah.

I don't usually feel the extra soul—I don't know what an additional soul is supposed to feel like exactly. Is it the downy inside of a soft sweatshirt? Is it in the crispiness of browned chicken skin? Is it a balm, like the cream I put on my pimples?

But when my father started singing "Yom Zeh L'Yisrael," soft at first, I did feel something. When he raised his voice and waved to the rest of us to join in, there was definitely something extra in the room. Whatever that thing was, it connected us, to God, but also to the rest of our people, the people we'd prayed with at the synagogue, our people back in Colwyn, our people in Israel, and all of the Jews who'd looked into the candlelight on their Shabbos tables over the centuries, and sung "Yom Zeh L'Yisrael," and felt at peace. I wondered if my graveyard pals, Cohen and Cantor, had sung this song. I wondered if they had nice voices.

Our peace lasted about a minute, until someone's phone dinged. We all looked around accusingly. The ding was sudden and brief, and nobody knew exactly where it had come from.

But then it dinged again.

And again.

And twice more.

"I don't think it's me," I said, because everybody was looking at me like it was me.

"Then why is the sound coming from your pocket?"

"Shut up, Chana. I'll kill you with my bare hands."

"You couldn't kill me with your bare hands."

"I could if you didn't resist."

"Why wouldn't I resist?"

It was me. It was my phone. My hand was in my pocket, itching and burning like it was on fire. I felt my fingers wrap around my phone. I felt them remove the phone from my pocket. I felt my eyes behold the phone as my hand held it out in front of me.

"On Shabbos, and at the *dinner* table no less," my dad said.

"We're not having dinner anymore," I replied. "So doesn't it revert back to being just the table?"

The problem was that we all knew who the text was from. A Jew wouldn't text on Shabbos. And it couldn't be spam, because spam doesn't text you four times in a row. It had to be Anna-Marie. It was like she'd invaded our Shabbos dining room, in flip-phone form. She was haunting the room like a ghost.

My father stared at my hand, rage quickly replacing the look of calm and peace he'd worn during his singing.

My mother looked back and forth between my hand and my father, taking her cue from him.

Zippy reached into my hand and plucked the phone away before I could open it—she was really *just* in time.

"I cannot believe you would do this," my father said, getting up from the table. He left his napkin next to his plate and disappeared from the room.

I didn't *do* anything. Receiving a text was passive, something that happened *to* me. But I did wish I'd remembered to turn my phone off, and to take it out of my pocket. I'd honestly forgotten it was in there. The rest of the family was looking at me, annoyed, and I understood it. I'd ruined a relaxing Shabbos meal.

But the worst part was that Anna-Marie had texted me and I couldn't look at what she said. If you were curating a customized torture for me, one designed to maximize my level of personal suffering, this is what you'd do: have Anna-Marie text me at the *beginning* of the Sabbath, then have my family give me the cold shoulder all weekend, so I had absolutely nothing to do but sit around wondering what Anna-Marie had said.

That's exactly what happened. And indeed I suffered.

Saturday morning services were the same as Friday evening's, just with more people. And then instead of doing stuff together as a family, we did everything alone. I tried to set myself up in the living room, so my family wouldn't have any excuse but to spend time with me. I even put some board games on the floor next to me, but nobody took me up on the offer. The younger sisters played upstairs. Zippy read in the kitchen. My mother sequestered herself in my parents' room. My father paced around like a caged animal, making huffing sounds, refusing eye contact. When I tried to wrestle Chana, she let herself go limp like a corpse, and just laid there on the floor. You know something's wrong if Chana won't engage in unnecessary violence.

So I just sat there and tortured myself by composing possible texts from Anna-Marie. They waffled back and forth between two extremes:

The outrageously pessimistic: Hoodie. It's Anna-Marie. I hate you. I never want to see you again. I hope that you meet a swift and painful end to your worthless existence. PS Starbursts are gross.

And the spectacularly optimistic: Hoodie. It's Anna-Marie. Secretly, I'm an Orthodox Jew. Surprise! Also, I love you. Also, I'm extraordinarily wealthy and after we marry, you, me, and our beautiful progeny will live a life of luxury wherein we spend most of our time relaxing on matching chaise lounges, while our servant Case feeds us various fine kosher cheeses on toothpicks, and we rate them for fun.

I wasn't sure what a chaise lounge was exactly, but it sounded fancy and included the word "lounge," so it had to be pretty good.

I wasn't a relationships expert, but I knew it was rude not to respond quickly to your girlfriend's texts. I tried to write responses in my head, as though that could somehow make up for it—maybe it was the thought that counted—but it was tough because I didn't know what she'd actually said.

On Saturday night, when there were three stars in the sky—or when the calendar on the kitchen wall said there were—we lit the Havdalah candle, blessed the wine, and passed around those sweet spices. When they got to me, I noticed they smelled extra sweet. They smelled like the return of my cell phone.

I met Zippy in her office, and she slipped me the phone under the kitchen table. "Be careful," she said.

I took the phone into my bedroom, carefully. I lay down on my bed, took a deep breath, and flipped the phone open.

There were five messages, all from Anna-Marie:

1. Hey Hoodie.

2. I'm sorry about what happened. I'm sorry about my friends. They suck sometimes.

3. Do you want to come over to my house on Sunday?

4. Hello?

5. [emoji that didn't come through properly due to the technological antiquity of my flip phone]

I sent back five texts in a flurry:

1. Hey Anna-Marie.

2. It's okay. My friends suck ALL the time.

3. Yes, I can come over on Sunday. I get out of school at 2.

4. It was the Sabbath. Couldn't text.

5. :)

CHAPTER 8

in which my lack of omniscience really lets me down

MY VISIT TO THE DIAZ-O'LEARY household was really bad timing, but I wouldn't know why until later that evening. The way people talked to me later, it was like they expected me to *feel* the antisemitism from a distance, like I was supposed to smell the bigotry in the air, or see it like a smoke signal. What exactly I should have done if I'd smelled it, they never said.

We have school on Sundays, but only Judaic studies, so we're done around two p.m. After school, my friends were going to walk down to the market to see if they could consume all of its snack food. I told them I was too tired to go with them.

"Yesterday was the Sabbath," Moshe Tzvi informed me. "That's the day of *rest*."

"Maybe at your house. Chana Rosen lives at mine."

I didn't know anybody who wasn't afraid of Chana. My

friends split off from me and walked toward town. I hung back a moment, pretending to read important text messages on my phone. Then I walked to Anna-Marie's house.

Borneo greeted me at the door.

I was pretty sure I'd never been in a gentile's house before. I wondered if they had all the same things. Did they have floors? What about walls? Did their stairs have bannisters, or did they just rely on their innate sense of balance?

I'm kidding about most of the above questions—I'd watched movies and TV, and their houses had all manner of walls. I'm just saying that I expected something significant to be different. If we were fundamentally different in the eyes of God, how could we live more or less the same way?

Anna-Marie's house was about the same as mine, just many times neater. You could walk around in her house without watching your step for hazards and obstacles—it was almost *too* easy. Her house was also brighter and somehow more modern, even though our houses were probably built at the same time. In my family's house, all of the furniture and decor was old and dark, like we lived in an ancient library. Even the books—the volumes of Jewish law and philosophy—were bound in dark reds and browns. But everything in the Diaz-O'Leary household was a light pastel color: the walls, the curtains, the furniture. They didn't have bookshelves in any public spaces. In their place they had big wooden signs that said stuff like THIS HOUSE RUNS ON LOVE AND LAUGHTER and HOME IS WHERE THE HEART IS.

The biggest difference between our two houses was that

Anna-Marie lived in this one. That's what I kept thinking about: *This* is the mat on which Anna-Marie leaves her shoes, which she removes from her feet. This is a chair that Anna-Marie sometimes sits on. This is a different chair that she sits on at other times. This is the refrigerator from which Anna-Marie retrieves her perishable foodstuffs.

Watching her dance on the internet was like looking through a window into her world. Now I'd climbed through that window and I was *in* that world, with her. I felt like one of those polar explorers, walking into a new frontier. Except that the polar explorers mostly starved and had to eat their own shoes.

Anna-Marie was wearing sweatpants and a hoodie. Her hair was pulled up in a scrunchie. She looked more at home than she had when we'd met on the street. I mean, she *was* at home, but she just looked more at ease.

Her mom appeared from around a corner. I expected her mom's entrance to be accompanied by some ominous music, like a movie villain. But there wasn't any music, and she didn't appear villainous. She was dressed more or less the same as her daughter, except her sweats weren't as colorful. Her hair was tied up in a neat bun, and she wore large glasses that took up a significant portion of her face.

The two of them didn't look much alike, actually. But then the mayor smiled and I saw the resemblance. She greeted me by mispronouncing my name in a few different ways. "Yay-*hoo*-dee," she said with a grin, combining my full name with my nickname and saying each syllable incorrectly.

When I interacted with non-Jews, I usually introduced myself as Judah. But Mrs. Diaz-O'Leary hadn't given me the opportunity, because she'd spoken first.

As she greeted me, she grinned and reached out her hand. Her smile faded when I didn't take it.

"Ma," Anna-Marie said. "He doesn't shake."

"Oh, I—"

"And just call him 'Hoodie,'" Anna-Marie said. "Like the sweatshirt. Repeat after me. Ready? Hoo—"

"Don't talk to me like that," her mom said.

We were off to a great start.

Hoping that another room would be less awkward, Anna-Marie's mom led us into the kitchen. I wasn't optimistic. Kitchens contain food. It was about lunchtime.

Anna-Marie sat down at the kitchen table. I stood in the doorway, just like I do in my own kitchen.

"I was going to make a sandwich. Can I make something for you guys?" Mrs. Diaz-O'Leary asked. "I've got tuna salad." She spent some time examining the package of bread. "Hey!" she said. "Look. It's kosher." And she held out the loaf to me like I was going to eat the plain bread from the bag just because it was kosher, like kosher food was rare and I just immediately consumed every calorie of kosher food I encountered.

"Ma, he's—"

"The tuna should be fine too so long as we don't melt any cheese—"

"No, Ma. You've touched the bread. You *made* the tuna salad in this kitchen."

"So?"

"You don't keep kosher. This isn't a kosher kitchen."

"It's tainted if I *touch* it?" she asked. She rolled her eyes, realized what she was doing, and tried to unroll them as fast as possible.

"Jesus, Ma. Facebook isn't the only app in the world. Can you not Google things? It's not hard."

Mrs. Diaz-O'Leary looked at me for confirmation that what her daughter was saying was true. I didn't really want to answer. Technically, if she'd used a new can opener, and all plastic cutlery, and an unopened bottle of kosher mayonnaise, I could probably have eaten that sandwich. But it didn't seem like the best time for an impromptu lesson on kashrut, and I didn't feel like I should have to personally defend the consistent three-thousand-year-old interpretation of God's law. So I just nodded.

The mayor looked at me as though, for her own comfort, I should be more flexible with God's commandments. She looked at Anna-Marie like her daughter was supposed to have given her a full briefing on my various proclivities. The tension in this kitchen was a lot like the tension in mine, just a slightly different flavor.

"I can eat non-kosher food if my life depends on it," I said. "So if you chain me up in your basement for a few weeks, I'll be able to eat anything you feed me."

This was, predictably I guess, not the right thing to say. Mother and daughter both looked at me, horrified.

"I wasn't saying you *would*. I just—what I'm saying is that I could eat anything, even bacon, if I would die without it."

"Ma won't let us have bacon, will you? Because it's not good for us."

"It's not," Mrs. Diaz-O'Leary said in a soft voice. It was a defeated voice. She leaned against the counter and muttered something about saturated fat. She blinked her eyes rapidly like she was trying not to cry. I couldn't be sure, though. Crying looks the same on most people, but *almost* crying always looks different depending on the person.

I really hoped she wouldn't cry. I wasn't an expert on relationships. But I was pretty sure when you met your girlfriend's parents, you weren't supposed to make them weep within the first five minutes.

"Jesus Christ," Anna-Marie said. "Let's get out of here, Hoodie."

Anna-Marie led me back through the hall toward the front of the house, then up the stairs. I knew which room was hers, because I'd seen the outside of her door in one of her videos. But I let her "show me" which one it was.

"I'm sorry, Hoodie," she said. "My mom is so embarrassing. So are my friends. So is my town. I feel like I'm apologizing every time I see you. You must think . . ."

But her voice trailed off before she could finish the thought. I wanted to assure her that I didn't think whatever it was I must think, but I didn't know what it was.

She opened the door to her room. It felt familiar: the forest-green curtains, the lime bedspread, the photos of friends tacked up on the white desk. Anna-Marie threw herself on her bed. There was no way I was going to sit on her bed. I eyed the only other seat in the room, a white swivel chair that matched the desk. But it was too deep in the room, so I just hung in the doorway, which ensured the door remained open, and I could tell myself—and I could tell God—that I wasn't actually going *into* her room.

Anna-Marie stared up at her ceiling. I tried to look anywhere but at her.

"Do you ever feel like nobody understands what you're going through?" Anna-Marie asked the ceiling.

"No," I said. But then I actually thought about it. "I mean, I *didn't* feel that way. Until recently. Now it happens every day. People are told how to live, how they're supposed to do things. And they do them that way because that's how they've always been done. But is that a good reason to do something? Is it wrong to ask why? There's a lot in the Gemara about how to treat slaves. But nobody has slaves anymore, because it's—well, it's self-explanatory. So now they say that we're supposed to interpret the slave stuff as a metaphor. Those Talmud passages, they're not about slave trade, they're just about commerce in general. But in order to make that change, somebody had to say, 'Wait. This slavery stuff is messed up. We need to see it differently.' Was that person a heretic? An apikores? Was that person exiled, put in cherem? Maybe he was, but then he turned out to be right. Am I breaking laws I *shouldn't* break, or am I the same as the person who pushed the Talmud slavery discussions into the metaphorical? Maybe I'll be recognized later as being right. Is that what you're saying?"

"Maybe? I didn't understand most of the words you just said. It's like, she talks about how hard it is for her, how working harder helps her heal. If she fights for the town, the town he grew up in, she can feel like she's protecting his memory. But that's *all* she can think about. It's taken over her whole life. What about *me*? She never asks me how *I'm* dealing with it. She never stops to think about how hard it is for *me*. And if I can't talk about it with her, who am I supposed to talk to? Case? My *friends*? What do they know? All they want to talk about is who's hooking up with who and trying to go viral on TikTok. I'd never go on social media again if I could . . . if he would just stand where you're standing one more time."

I figured she was talking about her dad. But I didn't know what to say. My dad was alive, and if he stood in my doorway, it meant I was in trouble.

"If nobody understands how you feel," she said, "you just feel . . . alone. I'm sitting on the couch with my mom. Or I'm hanging out with my friends. I'm with people, but I feel like I'm by myself, like I'm the only one in the world. Even when they look at me, I don't think they see me."

I actually did know that feeling. I was just getting acquainted with it, with all of the supposedly righteous people around me revealing their true colors. "I do know how that feels," I said. "I don't know about grief. But I know the other part."

"It sucks even more when the person you want to talk to the most is the only person you can't talk to."

I tried to think about what a good rabbi would say. "The Chofetz Chaim—he was like an O.G. Rabbi—had this thing about how we're just passing through this life, and—"

Anna-Marie was doing the same rapid blinking thing her mom had done. She got off her bed and walked toward me, her eyes red, her eyelids flying up and down. "I'm sorry, Hoodie. And I'm sorry for saying sorry again. I just need a hug."

I instinctively took a step backward, but before I knew it her hands were around me. Nothing horrible happened. It felt good. It felt safe.

"So hugs are, like, a reciprocal thing," Anna-Marie instructed. "It's easy. You just put your hands around the other person and squeeze."

I followed her directions.

I knew I was violating a commandment. I couldn't put my finger on which one, but I immediately started spinning it in my head, hoping that God was tuned in, listening. This was somebody who needed comfort, I told all the assembled in my mind. I wasn't having lewd thoughts about the hug. This wasn't a violation of the sanctity of the human body. This was providing a connection to somebody in need of one, and she was doing the same for me. Her sweatshirt had long sleeves and I wasn't touching any part of her bare skin.

When we parted, Anna-Marie looked less red. "How do you do that sound?"

Was I making a sound?

"That name you said."

"Chofetz Chaim."

"Yeah. Hofetz Haim."

"I'm not allowed to teach you. It's part of a secret code. I've sworn an oath."

"Really?"

"No. Ccchhhhh," I said. "It's in the middle of the mouth. Act like you're trying to cough something up, but make it vibrate more."

She tried it. It didn't go great. But the girl had perseverance. And even after a few coughing fits, she kept trying. "I got it. I got it," she said.

"No, you don't got it. You have a long way to go."

She pouted. But I could tell she wasn't really upset. "Let's practice downstairs," she said. "I think we do have food you can actually eat."

In the kitchen, she showed me an array of granola bars, individually packaged. And there was something else, a pack of Starburst. I was about to tell her that they weren't kosher, but she put on a British accent and said, "These, mate, are from the United Kingdom." She'd gotten them from the Abramowitz market. "Actually," she said, "British Starburst are better."

We took our bounty to the couch, and then we sat around and watched TV. With the TV on, we didn't have to say anything. TV was universal. We just sat there, staring at the flashing images, feeling not-alone. We sat at opposite ends of the couch, but it still felt like we were together. Every so often we'd look across at each other and smile.

I loved the way she looked at me, like I was the only person who existed, like I was the only person she *needed* to exist, at least in that moment. She locked her dark brown eyes with mine and just kept them there, resting, like she was happy to just gaze at me for as long as I wanted to gaze back—which was, you know, a long time.

The second date was going even better than the first, and not just because this one was air-conditioned.

In the early evening, we took Borneo out for a walk. He peed on things, including our tree, *the* tree, the one at which I'd met Anna-Marie back on Tu B'Av. I wished I'd had one of Moshe Tzvi's many knives with me. We could have carved our initials into the tree. It could have been our secret: H + A-M. Something like that, something nobody but us would understand.

The weather was finally starting to turn. The breeze that blew through the neighborhood was cool. Fall peeked at us from around a corner. Anna-Marie was talking about going back to school—she was super psyched about it. I'm kidding. She was the opposite of that.

"I wish I could just walk out of school," she said. "We could take walks together. You know, for self-reflection."

"Mutual reflection."

"Yeah," Anna-Marie said with a half-smile. "I like reflecting with you. There's this . . . lack of pressure. We don't know any of the same people. You won't tell anybody what I said. I don't know. I feel like I can be honest with you in a way that I can't with other people."

"I'm going to relay this conversation to Case verbatim."

She gave me a playful punch in the shoulder. "Oh yeah? How are you going to do that? You going to call the operator with your rotary phone and ask them to look up his number in the directory?"

"That's really a low blow. Some things have to be off-lim—"

Speaking of phones, mine buzzed. I almost cursed out loud. The text was almost certainly a call back to the other part of my life. But I wanted to stay here in this part, H + A-M + little Borneo, the island dog.

I flipped up my phone. The text was from Zippy. Get away from her RIGHT NOW, the text said. Get to the market ASAP. Sneak in. Use the back door. Act like you've been there the whole time. Do it now.

I instinctively jumped back from Anna-Marie, then looked around me, half expecting Zippy to be lurking somewhere, à la Moritz in the cemetery. But there was nobody there.

"You all right?" Anna-Marie asked.

"Yeah," I said. "I just—I have to go."

"Okay," she said. I was hoping she'd sound disappointed. But her voice was flat, inscrutable.

Zippy's text was clearly urgent, so I just started walking away. Then jogging. Then running. I hustled down the main drag, then hooked up the hill toward the bridge that went over the tracks. I cut down an alley into the narrow parking lot between the main business strip and the train tracks—it ran parallel to the two.

Out of habit, I was about to rap my fingers on the back door of the market, but I stopped myself just in time. I slowly and quietly pulled the door open and slipped inside. I guided the door silently back into its place.

Even from the storeroom, I could hear voices, lots of them. The store had to be absolutely packed.

As soon as the market opened last fall, it became the de facto community meeting place. It was the only truly Jewish place in town, other than the synagogue. Back in Colwyn, we owned all the stores, restaurants, community centers. Everywhere you went, you were with your people. It felt like you were always among family. But here, the Abramowitz Family Kosher Market was our only spot. That's where my buddies and I met up to test the human limits of Doritos consumption. That's where my little sisters got together to chase my friends' little sisters in circles at high speed. That's where our mothers got together to gossip about their marriages, and their kids' marriages. That's where our dads got together to bow their heads together and talk business and Jewish law.

Also, the market could fit more people than the synagogue, which is why the whole community met up there after the incident that day.

There were plastic flaps separating the storeroom from the main part of the market. I poked my head through. With the high-rise on hold, I didn't realize there were enough of us here to fill the store, but we filled it. The aisles were absolutely packed. People stood shoulder to shoulder to halva box, pressed against each other and the merchandise.

The only place where there was open space was behind the checkout/deli counter. Behind the glass of the deli display there were various community leaders: Rabbi Friedman, Mr. Abramowitz, my father. Next to them, behind the cash register, stood Dr. Reznikov, and next to him stood three of my classmates: Reuven Miller, Chaim Abramowitz, Moshe Tzvi Gutman.

But my classmates weren't in their usual tip-top shape. Reuven was sporting a spectacular black eye. It had as many colors as Joseph's coat. To the untrained eye, Moshe Tzvi looked normal. But Moshe Tzvi is like a wild animal who will hide weakness at all costs, so as not to alert predators to his weakened state. And I could tell by the way he was standing that he'd hurt his shoulder or arm. He was just the slightest bit off-kilter, leaning a little to his left, his jaw set in a grimace. Chaim looked fine—both of his arms were still fractured in a record number of places, obviously—but he was intently watching his father.

Mr. Abramowitz had Chaim's kippah in his hand and was holding it up in front of the crowd. The kippah was Chaim's favorite. It was classy, made of suede, trimmed with silver thread. But now it was torn down the middle, almost in half. The silver trim was the only thing still holding it together.

I took a sudden sharp breath.

A few people at the back of the crowd snapped around and saw me peeking in from the storeroom.

I tried to play it cool. I stepped into the market, and pretended to check my fly, like I'd just used the bathroom. But I could tell from their looks of recognition and anger that they didn't buy my excuse.

After about a minute inside the market, I figured out what had happened.

When we got out of school, I went to Anna-Marie's. My friends went to the market. They got some snacks—popcorn, Starburst, Elite Doritos—green bag, sour and spicy flavor, imported from Israel.

My friends were walking around, snacking, enjoying the weather, enjoying the eliteness of their Doritos, when they were confronted by a group of local kids. The local delinquents shouted antisemitic slurs, and when my classmates took issue with the verbal abuse, the kids transitioned to physical abuse and attacked my friends.

At one point, two of the hoodlums were holding Chaim against a wall. They wondered aloud if Chaim wore his fedora to cover his Jew horns. So they took off his hat. When the hat removal didn't reveal any horns, they thought maybe the horns were just really small, and were covered by Chaim's kippah. So they removed that too. When Chaim's head was still without horns, they tore the kippah almost in half, but stopped and ran when a passerby saw them and started shouting.

I suddenly felt queasy. I put a hand on a shelf to keep myself steady. What had I told my dad? I'd said that this kind of thing wouldn't happen here. And it would have happened to *me*, if I hadn't had my date with Anna-Marie.

Rabbi Friedman was talking, using the cash register in place of a shtender or podium. Rabbi Friedman was the leader of the congregation, as well as the top local rabbi at the school. He had a long gray beard and potbelly. He always swayed backward and forward when he spoke. He had a soft voice, but still it carried through the market. It was clear from the fatigue on his face that he'd been talking for a while. He was wrapping up. "We've known what it is to live in exile since the fall of the first temple. We all know what it is to fight this battle. The hate pains us. It affronts us as it affronts God. But it also affirms our belief that through our traditions, through our congregation's support, through the many wonders of HaShem, we will keep ourselves safe here. Now, I have been speaking with Mr. Rosen, Mr. Abramowitz, and Dr. Reznikov—and we've spoken with Rabbi Taub—about practical matters. For those, I will turn the proceedings over to Mr. Rosen."

My father took a step forward. He stood tall. He could put on a commanding persona when he wanted to: for board meetings, legal hearings, readings at synagogue. "I've spoken to local law enforcement," he said. "Predictably, they've shirked their responsibility to protect *all* of their constituents. They listened, but it was clear that they will do nothing. So, as we're accustomed to doing, we will take care of ourselves. The plan is as follows. Nobody will travel alone, even adults. If you are driving, fine. But if you are walking, you must walk in groups of at least two. For all school-age children, we will assign adults, based on location, to accompany them to and from school each day. We know that we are all busy, and this will be a *heavy* lift. However, we're doing this for our children, for our community, for our people, for our future. We will lock the synagogue doors during prayers and keep two people at the door at all times. In the meantime, Rabbi Friedman and I will appeal to the mayor, town council, and police for an easing of tension. If anything good can come of this, it could be that our legal standing will improve, as our persecution here is now manifest, undeniable, embodied in the physical and emotional suffering of our—"

My father was interrupted by a rapping on the glass window of the store. Heads all turned toward the street side of the market, where five police officers stood. The lead one, the one who'd rapped, tapped his foot and beckoned with his hand.

"Excuse me," my father said to the crowd. The audience parted for him and Rabbi Friedman as they made their way outside. They jingled through the door and stood on the sidewalk with the officers.

The lead officer spoke, his mouth moving quickly. As he spoke, he shook his index finger at the assembled crowd. The other officers shifted their weight impatiently.

In response to whatever the officer was saying, both Rabbi Friedman and my father threw their hands up in the air.

Now there was an argument happening, but none of us could hear it. The faces of both sides reddened, and everybody was gesticulating at the inside of the market, nodding, pointing, waving at us. Rabbi Friedman was spitting mad, stamping his right foot on the ground as he spoke, his too-big suit jacket flying around in all directions as his bobbing head threatened to toss his hat into the air.

After a minute or so, my dad and the rabbi came back inside, shaking their heads. They walked to the counter.

Out on the street, the officers stood in a little circle, conferring.

Rabbi Friedman cleared his throat and was about to speak, but the officers had made their decision.

They opened the front door. The lead officer pushed his way inside. "*You're* doing this," the officer called out to the rabbi. "We gave you the chance to do the right thing. This assembly endangers the community and violates the fire code."

"Don't tell me about danger to *my* community," Rabbi Friedman said.

The officer ignored him and addressed the crowd. "Everybody out," he said. "Now."

We all looked up at Rabbi Friedman for direction. "Stay where you are," he said. "This is *our* place. Do not let this oyev, this soneh, this enemy, come into—"

"Now!" the officer shouted. Then he turned to the officer next to him, and said, "Can you believe these people? The rules apply to everybody. Why can't they get it through their heads?"

Up front, my father looked at the ground. Rabbi Friedman looked up at the ceiling, or the heavens through the ceiling.

Nobody moved. We all stood stock-still, unsure what to do. The police were telling us their law said one thing, and the rabbi was telling us that God's law said the other. It was exactly what Anna-Marie had told me on the way to the hardware store:

there were two groups of people here, each following their own set of rules.

This situation was basically the whole thing—the entire fight between Tregaron and our community—distilled down into one moment. There was something almost embarrassing about it, that all these distinguished leaders couldn't work something out. Goldie and Rivkie were better at resolving conflict, and they could barely dress themselves without help.

As if to illustrate my point, the top officer suddenly reached out and grabbed the nearest person, Mrs. Gutman, by the arm. She shrieked, and tried to pull away, but we were packed in tight, so as she turned she crashed into her daughter, who in turn knocked over a display of crackers, which in turn knocked over Mrs. Goldberg. As she tumbled to the floor, Mrs. Goldberg's sheitel fell off her head, exposing her hair.

This was the type of slapstick I usually enjoyed, but I was horrified. You didn't just reach out and touch women's bodies.

Another officer reached down and offered a hand to Mrs. Goldberg, but she didn't take it. She was reaching around on the floor among all the feet, looking for her sheitel. The officer grabbed her by both arms and pulled her up off the floor. She writhed in his arms as he dragged her outside.

My father was shouting now, and Rabbi Friedman was talking too, but I couldn't hear either of them. The place was all noise and chaos, like the Rosen household when the girls have access to Popsicles.

The police were grabbing anybody they could reach and

dragging them out onto the street, shouting and cursing as they did so.

Everybody saw the writing on the proverbial wall and started making their way outside, but there was only one door, so there was a squeeze as they tried to make their way out at the same time the police were dragging their friends and family by force.

I took the back door again, hustled up the parking lot and all the way around the strip of connected shops. I approached the crowd from up the street.

We were all spilled out on the sidewalk now, but there wasn't enough room, and a bunch of us were in the street, blocking traffic. Horns blared, adding sound to the light show—the police cars that idled out front had their lights on, spinning shadows onto the buildings in the early evening light.

The main officer stood next to the door, his face bright red, sweat dripping off his chin. He had his finger almost up against Mr. Abramowitz's nose, and I could just hear his voice over the car horns: "The store is *closed* for today. Do you hear me? Do you *hear* me? *Closed.*"

Mr. Abramowitz had the key in his hand but he was still protesting, his arms shrugging up and down as he spoke. But when the officer reached out to take the keys himself, Mr. Abramowitz put up a hand as if to say, "Okay, okay," and he locked the door.

The officers made their way back to their vehicles, gesturing for the crowd to disperse. We broke off into little fragments, walking slowly up the hill on the sidewalk and in the street.

My mind and heart were racing, and the latter was aching too, with a new kind of pain. I was in disbelief. I couldn't believe what I'd just seen. Sure, nobody had had to cut off their toes. But other than that, how different was this from the pogroms back in my great-grandparents' shtetl? They had law enforcement target us when *we* were the ones who were attacked.

I found myself walking in a group with the Gutmans and Goldbergs. Mrs. Goldberg's face was white as a sheet, but somebody had provided her a cloth to wrap her head with. I looked at her to offer sympathy.

But the look I got in return was not acceptance of sympathy. Her eyes narrowed when she recognized me. "Yehuda Rosen," she said, and she shook her head at me. "What kind of young man are you?" she asked.

I had no idea what she was getting at. Maybe she was just disturbed, understandably, by the police brutality. "What kind of Jewish boy treats his parents the way you are treating yours?" she went on. "What kind of Jewish man can you be if you treat your parents this way? Turning yourself from them, *and* from God. If you were my son, I wouldn't even look you in the eye. I wouldn't *let* you shame me the way you are shaming your father and mother."

I looked down at myself, trying to see if I noticed anything that would induce shame.

But Mrs. Gutman jumped in to help out. "He violates God's commandments, and he does it with *that shiksa*. It is sinister, like he has chosen just the most painful, humiliating way to rub his sin in *all* of our faces. And on this of all days, while his people are under attack, where is he? Where is the son of Mr. Rosen? I can't even *bring* myself to . . ."

When I say that she "helped," I mean only that she explained what it was that Mrs. Goldberg was talking about.

I couldn't bring myself to respond to them, so I split off from their group and joined another, but I got the same treatment there. It wasn't the furtive, disapproving glances of the Shabbos services. This was open hostility, fury.

I set aside the question of how they knew. I'd been out walking with Anna-Marie. It only took one set of eyes to see me.

I tried to walk up to the Reznikov family. They were walking on the sidewalk, spread out. But when I approached, they closed rank. Dr. Reznikov glared at me. He watched me out of the corner of his eye. When I got within earshot, he said, "Your poor father. He works hard for us. He does not deserve this."

I rebounded into the street, like a ball bouncing back off a wall. I walked alone, feeling deflated, discarded.

As we neared home and the crowd thinned, I found Zippy and Yoel. Yoel saw me coming over his shoulder. He grimaced through his well-trimmed beard, but he knew Zippy wouldn't send me away. He split off from her and crossed the street to walk with a friend. I glided into step with my sister.

We walked in silence for a minute.

"I tried," she said.

"I know."

"Think, Hoodie. *Think.* This can get really bad for you, *really* bad. It might be too late."

"People are more pissed at me than they are at the kids who beat them up."

"That surprises you? You're such a fast-talker, but sometimes you're so thickheaded. You should be thankful they'll look at you long enough to give you the stink eye."

"Thank you for that comforting—"

"I'm not interested in comforting you. You have to understand that expectations of you are fundamentally different than they are for *them.* The community's expectations, *God's* expectations."

When Zippy said "them," I thought back to Anna-Marie's house. Sure, the color scheme was different, but the chairs and granola and relationships in their house felt just like ours. "I don't know," I said. "When you really think about it, aren't we all—"

"The same? No. God set us apart. *We* are the people he gave his Torah to. You're bearing the brunt of this because they don't expect this from you. They expect it from non-Jews. Gentiles have treated Jews poorly in the past, and they expect that to continue. They've seen that story play out over and over, and they expect it to play out again and again. That's why—well, it's one of the reasons—we stick together like this," she went on, waving her hand to indicate our big crowd. "Because we know that in this hostile world, we can rely on each other. But if you show your people that they *can't* rely on you, well, it's the ultimate betrayal."

As my astute sister Zippy noted on our lovely stroll back from the market, I am a "fast-talker." But when we got home, I did no talking. I didn't even need my lawyer to advise me to invoke my Fifth Amendment rights.

My father spoke to me for about a minute. I don't think he could bring himself to talk to me in the house, so he had me wait outside on the stoop while the rest of the family trooped inside.

He refused to make eye contact with me. We stood outside in the dying light. He gazed up over my shoulder at the horizon. I heard a window open above, and knew Chana was coming out onto the roof. I was hoping she'd dump something on us, but no projectile was forthcoming.

"I won't be able to look my colleagues in the eye tomorrow, Yehuda. What will I say to our community at the synagogue? What will they think at the town council? What ground will I have to stand on? This is what you've done to me. You bring this shame upon us. Why?" he asked. "Why? A man gives his life to serve his God, to serve his community, and his son thinks only of himself. Why?"

I was going to respond, but it became clear he wasn't even talking to me. He was looking past me, through me, around me.

"My only son. Why, Lord? What is the purpose of this? In this new and foreign place my only son turns from us?"

I was almost as tall as he was, and I was starting to fill out just a little. I wondered if he could carry me up a mountain. If he could get me up there, I was now certain he'd be willing to go through with his sacrifice. If it meant he could build his high-rise, if it meant he could string up his eruv, he'd spill my blood.

I stepped toward the door.

"You will not see that shiksa again," he said quietly, talking to the blood-red horizon. "You will go nowhere but school and home. You will keep your door open at all times, and when I walk by your room, I will see you with a Gemara in your hands. You will bring no more shame on us."

He reached out his hand to me. At first I thought he wanted me to shake, but his palm was turned upward.

I knew what he was doing but pretended not to.

"Now," he muttered. "You won't need it. You'll be at school, or you'll be at home."

"Moshe Tzvi gets Talmud lessons by text. There's a number you can message and they send you Gemara discussions and—"

"No."

I reached into my pocket. I opened the phone to send Anna-Marie an explanation text, but he slid it out of my fingertips.

Now he stepped toward the door and went inside. He closed the door behind him. I just looked at the closed door, wondering if I was even allowed in. I half expected to hear the dead bolt lock behind him.

"How long do you think it would take me to build a doghouse big enough to sleep in?" I asked the porch ceiling.

I couldn't see her, but I could sense Chana's presence on the roof above me. "Do you want me to lend you one of my hammers?" she asked.

"No, I was only—wait, where did you get multiple hammers?"

"No comment."

I could picture her up there, seated with her knees pulled up to her chest. I wished I could go join her. We could just sit quietly and watch the sun go down together. But I guessed that wouldn't have been safe. It's probably refreshing to dip yourself in the cool waters of the Amazon River, right up until the piranhas start pulling the flesh off your legs.

"I'm really sorry, Hoodie."

Maybe Chana was changing a bit as she got older, growing a soft spot. "Sorry for what?" I asked.

"You'll see."

Okay, maybe not.

"But I really am sorry."

CHAPTER 9

in which there are antisemitic hashbrowns

I TRIED TO SLEEP. BUT sleep is one of those things where success has an inverse relationship to effort. The harder you try to sleep, the less likely you are to actually accomplish it. It was difficult to sleep with the door open, but that was somewhere near the bottom of the extensive list of sleep-resistant issues. I was thinking about my dad, God, Anna-Marie, the attack on my friends.

I'd felt so at home on the couch with Anna-Marie, and now I felt like an outsider in my own house.

No matter how many wild asses I counted, no matter how many times I said, "Okay, Hoodie, nighty night now, buddy," no matter how many times Leah asked through the wall, "Why are you talking to yourself, you weird creep?" I was still wide awake.

Sometime in the middle of the night, I got up and walked down to the kitchen. I told myself I was getting a snack, but I wasn't hungry.

Zippy was asleep with her head on the table, her long hair spread out in all directions. The laptop was closed on the table next to her. I pulled a chair out for myself and flipped the computer open.

I wanted to send a message to Anna-Marie, to let her know what happened. I couldn't text her. I couldn't call her from the landline because her number was in my phone. What if she texted me? I wouldn't be able to reply. What would she think? Would she think I didn't like her? That I was dumping her? It was physically painful just to think about it. I needed to get a message to her somehow.

I pulled up the page where she posted the dance videos. There was a dance video from the day before, but I didn't watch it, because there was a new video from tonight. I could tell from the little preview that she wasn't dancing in this one. I clicked on it.

Anna-Marie's face was close to the camera. She looked pale, and there were dark rings around her eyes. She spoke to the camera in a quiet, ragged voice. "As I'm sure some of you guys heard, something . . . happened tonight. And I—I just wanted to say that it's *not* okay. I know it's cheesy in school when they tell us to celebrate diversity and appreciate differences and all that. But it's true. I made a new friend—I won't say his name—and it's true. You really do learn from people who are different from you. When you see somebody who's not like you, don't push away. Reach out. You might—you might learn something. That's . . . that's all I wanted to say. Sorry I got serious. I still got more dashes than all y'all. Hyphens out."

The video was heartwarming. It was *too* heartwarming. My whole chest was on fire. I felt like I was going to turn to ash. My dad would come downstairs in the morning and ask, "Where's Hoodie?" And Zippy would be like, "Hoodie? Oh, he's just a pile of ash now. Yeah, don't sit on the chair, you'll get him on your pants."

Next to the video there were a bunch of those hash things. Hashtags? Hashbrowns? Okay, I knew it was hashtag, but hashbrowns are so delicious. Under the hashtags, there were links to a couple of news articles. One of them was from the local newspaper, but two of them were from big news websites, ones that were read all over the country. I clicked on one of them.

It said that there had been an attack on youths of the "burgeoning" Orthodox Jewish community in Tregaron. The suspects got away. Later, the Jewish community held an illegal meeting at a kosher market, where they burgeoned so much, the police had to break up the gathering for safety reasons. The article had a quote from the mayor. "We need to ask the members of our Jewish community to follow important regulations, such as the fire code," she said. "When we have three times the legal capacity in a space, it endangers the entire downtown district, the whole town. Tregaronites are welcoming people. All we ask is that all of our residents respect our community values and look out for everybody's well-being." Monica Diaz-O'Leary didn't mention the attack at all.

They'd just beaten up Moshe Tzvi, and torn up Chaim's kippah, and she was telling *us* to "respect" the community? Her message couldn't have been more different from her daughter's. I was with my dad on one thing: Anna-Marie's mom was the worst.

I made the mistake of scrolling down below the article where there were comments. I read exactly three of them:

1. "This is how it starts. How will it end? Watch my video. #jewsdid911" This was followed by a link to a video that I can only assume proved the commenter's point.

2. "These things swarm like roaches. The final solution should have been final. Heil Hitler!"

3. "Another hoax from the zionist parasites. They rough themselves up, cry foul. Wake up! There's still time to stop the jewish invasions. #holohoax #holocaustwasalie #soros"

I snapped the laptop shut after the third comment, then opened it and slowly read them again, double-checking that they were real. The comments made me want to laugh. The Holocaust was verifiably real. And the Zionist takeover was even more ludicrous. There were twelve million Jews in the whole world. There were more Rwandans than Jews, more Yankees fans, more people who had congenital birth defects that caused them to have eleven toes. Could you imagine if people were out there railing against conspiratorial world dominance by the extra-toe people, how ridiculous that would be?

But anyway, I didn't laugh. Because there were some messed-up people out there. I sat in shock at the antisemitism and in love with Anna-Marie's earnest plea for love and acceptance. Then I felt myself drifting off. I shook myself out of the chair and got upstairs just in time to collapse into my bed.

CHAPTER 10

in which I become a princess, kind of

WHEN I WOKE UP AND looked out the window, it was just light enough to distinguish Yoel Berger from a wild ass. He stood at the curb alone, leafing through a book.

Yoel is one of these aloof book people. Most of what he does is stand around leafing through books. He's like a book himself: he looks nice, and smells okay, but when you get to know him, he's horrifically boring.

Zippy loves him more than he loves books. There was a phase when she wouldn't talk about anything but Yoel. You could be like, "Yo, Zip. Do we have any Frosted Flakes?"

And she'd be like, "Yoel's face is frosted. With stubble, like a fresh dusting upon the well-manicured lawn of an elegant manor. I can't wait to feel his stubbled cheek against mine." And she would put her hand to her own cheek, pretending it was Yoel's face.

Chana solved this problem. Any time Zippy talked about Yoel, Chana would make a series of more and more intense simulated vomiting sounds, until one time she actually made herself throw up. It was a top five moment of my life, Chana standing over her own vomitus in triumph, me laughing maniacally, Leah covering her eyes and retching, Zippy just sitting there, chagrined, because she knew it was her fault.

In quieter moments, I would ask Zippy what she actually liked about Yoel. "What's interesting about him? He never *says* anything. He's just this thin silent blob. He's like a root vegetable. He's basically a carrot."

"He's just . . . He's special. He makes me feel special."

"Can you describe this special feeling?"

"No. It would be a problem if I could describe it. It's not supposed to be describable. It's like God in that way. It is written that my husband will be the other half of my soul. I am half without him, but when I'm with him, I can feel the other half of myself. The Talmud says that when we wed, when our names come together, we will spell one of the names of HaShem."

I made fun of her, obviously—as her brother, I was contractually obligated to do so. But now that I had my own girlfriend, I knew how she felt. I couldn't put my finger on what was special about Anna-Marie. But every time I thought about her, I just filled up with a strange tingling inside. She made me feel warm and safe, but then she also elevated my heart rate in a way that was uncomfortable. But it was a *good* kind of discomfort, the best kind, the kind you never want to go away.

Just thinking those thoughts as I got out of bed, I half expected to hear Chana retching through the wall.

I met Yoel at the curb. "Where's everybody else?" I asked him. My understanding was that we were going to walk to school in groups.

"Good morning, Hoodie," he said, and started walking.

He walked as though I weren't with him, as though he were alone in the world, or alone *not* in the world. He continued reading as he strolled, looking up now and then to make sure he wasn't about to crash into anything. He mumbled to himself as he read, as though conducting his own internal lesson. Every so often he would say something to me. "Getting deeper into Rabbi Shimon's philosophy is making me rethink some of the halachic understandings I've long held. I wonder if it will do the same for you. As a yeshiva student, I thought of him primarily in terms of the Zohar, but there's so much more. He's a treasure trove."

"You don't say. Wow. Everybody loves a good trove." I had no idea what else to say. I had barely understood the page we'd reviewed in yesterday's Gemara class.

If I was the worst nightmare of the Jewish parent—lacking devotion, without talent and interest in Talmud—Yoel was the ideal son. Yoel was so devoted to his studies that he couldn't be bothered to put them on hold even for basic life necessities, like safe personal locomotion. If they made waterproof Talmuds, the dude would read them in the shower. On their wedding night, when he and Zippy went back to their new place, she would reach out to touch his stubble, and he would reach for the obscure works of Rabbi Shimon bar Yochai and start a debate about inscrutable midrash. Though now that I'm thinking about it, Zippy would be super into that.

Yoel walked right by the school. I almost kept walking with him to see when he would notice—maybe when the sun went down and he couldn't see the page anymore? But I didn't want to miss Shacharis. I was in trouble enough already.

Before I even got to the beis medrash, it became immediately clear why I'd been the only student walking with Yoel. None of my classmates would come anywhere near me. They wouldn't make eye contact with me. I repelled them like we were of opposite magnetic charges. Or the same magnetic charges? Whichever pushes away.

I should have brought a spittoon with me, because kids made mock spitting noises when they walked by me. The bolder ones would whisper something passive-aggressive along with their fake spit. They called me "apikores," "kofer ba-ikkar," and some other names I couldn't quite hear. Reuven Miller "accidentally" bumped into me right outside the beis medrash. He did it with his elbow out. It caught me just under the ribs, and knocked the wind out of me.

I stood against the wall just outside the beis medrash, trying to catch my breath, feeling a combination of bone bruise and betrayal. I'd known every one of these kids since we were in diapers. And now they were looking at me like they didn't recognize me, or like they wished they didn't.

In the beis medrash, I placed my hat on my hook, and grabbed my tefillin bag. I went to take my regular seat next to Moshe Tzvi. Moshe Tzvi was wrapping his arm-tefillin around his wrist, but when he noticed me he stopped and slid down two seats, away from me.

I tried to shoot him a look, but he wouldn't meet my eyes. Just to test it out, I inched closer to him, but he inched away. "Moshe Tzvi," I whispered, "I—"

But he made an almost imperceptible motion with his lower jaw that cut me off. I wanted to try again—I couldn't have him turn from me—but Rabbi Friedman was about to begin the service, and I needed to suit up.

Tefillin are gear you put on for morning prayers. They go on your head and arm. It's kind of like putting on pads before you play a contact sport, except that, as far as I know, football helmets don't contain little boxes with Torah verses in them.

Usually I gear up and pray at the same pace as everybody else, moving through the service along with Moshe Tzvi, even synchronizing our swaying to and fro. But this morning I dawdled, took my time, drawing it out. This way I wouldn't have to walk out of the beis medrash with everyone else. By the time my tefillin were back in their bag, the only people left were me, Rabbi Moritz, and Rabbi Friedman. I felt good about this until they appeared to also feel good about it.

They slowly made their way across the carpet toward me. They met me at my hat peg. Rabbi Friedman plucked my Borsalino off its peg and handed it to me. Rabbi Moritz said, "Come with us, Yehuda."

"Sure," I agreed, as though I had a choice.

I followed them out of the beis medrash onto the walkway that led to the old stone yeshiva building. I followed a couple paces behind them, trying to make it look like I wasn't walking *with* them—I was out for a stroll by myself and the rabbis just happened to be on the same walkway. Just before we stepped into the main building, I looked up at the classroom windows, at dozens of beady eyes, watching me with a combination of derision and curiosity. I've read that in some countries, people still attend public executions. I imagine the people who show up to watch one of those stare at the condemned the same way my classmates were staring at me.

The classrooms were on the ground floor of the old church building. Rabbis Moritz and Friedman led me up the winding wooden staircase that led to the dark, musty offices of the upper floors. The stairs squeaked and groaned with each of our steps. We passed the second floor where the main office was located, then the third floor where Rabbi Friedman had his office. We stopped on the fourth-floor landing. Above us there was a hole in the ceiling that led to the belfry. There was a rickety ladder you could climb to ring the bell, though I'd never heard it ring. There was also a single door, which led into a little room.

Moritz motioned for me to open the door.

"Am I going to have to get a hunched back?" I asked him.

He said nothing.

"That was a joke. It's the plot of a book. This outcast dude lives at the top of a church and his back is all messed up. At the end, he dies of starvation. It's an uplifting tale. I recommend—"

"Yehuda."

"Yes, Rebbe."

"Inside."

"Yes, Rebbe."

The room contained a single wooden desk, a single wooden chair, and a tiny square window with frosted glass. If not for the sliver of light that sneaked through the glass, you would have thought it was a dungeon.

"Please take a seat."

"You mean *the* seat."

Moritz said nothing. I took the seat.

"Rabbi Friedman will wait with you," Moritz said.

Moritz left the room. I could hear his footsteps on the stairs, descending.

"I regret that this is necessary," Rabbi Friedman said. Unlike Moritz, Rabbi Friedman usually suppressed his anger. If he was angry at you, it came out looking like sadness. His eyes got a little watery. "Your presence, your situation, will provide an unnecessary distraction to your classmates," he continued. "We cannot take the chance that you will pass your ill-gotten, ill-conceived thinking on to others. A yeshiva student has enough challenges as one of God's men already."

Just like Moritz, Rabbi Friedman spoke about my "situation" like it was an illness I'd contracted, a virulent infection my classmates could catch through the air. If I was exposed to the rest of the population, we could have an epidemic on our hands. We'd all be strolling around the campus in shorts and tank tops with bikini-clad shiksas on our arms, listening to licentious pop music on our new smartphones.

"Can you tell me where I actually went 'wrong'?" I asked. "Was it when I defended the sanctity of the desecrated headstones? Or was it when I happened to *not* get assaulted for my religion?"

Friedman didn't respond. He probably didn't think they were real questions, which was fair—they likely sounded sarcastic, because I'm me. And maybe I wasn't actually confused about what I'd done "wrong." I was dating the evil mayor's daughter, and the way they saw it, I'd crossed over to the wrong side of the turf war. But what I didn't understand was how it had gotten this bad this quickly. And what would happen to me if I couldn't get back?

In the hot, stuffy room, a chill ran down my spine. "I'm going to fall behind in math and language arts," I said, and because nobody cared about those, I added, "and Gemara."

Friedman dismissed these trivialities with a wave of his hand. "I have spoken to Rabbi Taub. He has agreed to come speak with you, Rabbi Taub. This is an honor, to speak personally to Rabbi Taub. He is a great and wise man, Rabbi Taub. You will remain in this room until he arrives later this week, with God's help."

I wanted to be snarky with Rabbi Friedman, but you couldn't. It didn't work on him. He was impervious to it. He didn't experience humor, and he had none of the vulnerability of the younger Rabbi Moritz.

The younger rabbi appeared once more in the doorway, holding a stack of books. Four of them were Talmud volumes. Another was a notebook. From his pocket he produced a pen and a slip of paper.

"Yehuda, you have committed a chet *and* a pesha. You have sinned against HaShem, for which you must do teshuvah and repent. You have also sinned against your fellow Jews, against your friends, your family, your people. You will have to ask their forgiveness."

I could agree that *maybe* I'd sinned against God with Anna-Marie, but I didn't see how I'd wronged my friends or family. I also didn't see how it was a pesha, since I didn't do any of it out of rebelliousness. "It's not a pesha, Rebbe," I told him.

"Of course it's a pesha. Clear as day it is a pesha."

Rabbi Moritz put the slip of paper down in front of me. It had a list of pages and Talmud passages on it. "You will study these pages, and you will copy these passages into this notebook until it is full. If you read with clarity, you will understand what you have done, and the path to teshuvah, to repentance, God willing. You may leave the room for lunch and for prayers only."

"Do you have, like, a bucket I can pee in?"

"For the bathroom you may leave as well."

When they left the room, I was ready to do an actual pesha and leave the Gemaras unopened on the table. But there was nothing else to do in my little prison room, so I opened the first volume. I had a lot of trouble figuring out what the first page was saying. My Hebrew reading is poor, and I couldn't really get at the meaning.

I wished Moshe Tzvi were there. He always gave me quick run-throughs before Gemara quizzes.

I guessed I could copy the passages into the notebook without actually knowing what they meant, so I got started on that.

After a couple pages my wrist hurt, and I got up and went to the window. I tried to look out, but the glass was clouded and I could only make out distant colors: the green of the grass, the blue of the sky.

I went back to my pages. The boredom and monotony were excruciating. I realized I didn't even know what time it was, since my dad had confiscated my phone.

I felt like a princess in a fairy tale, trapped in a tower with no clock or cell phone, surrounded by monsters. If only Prince Charming would come rescue me. I supposed Moshe Tzvi would have to be my Prince Charming—there weren't any other candidates. He wouldn't make a good prince. Ideally, you don't want your prince to be a pimpled, nose-picking pedant. But at a certain point anyone will do. And I didn't expect him to come anyway, the way he'd treated me at Shacharis.

I was staring out the little window, trying to see if I could pick out any blurry trees, when there was a knock on the door. I assumed it was Rabbi Moritz, come to check up on me. But it was Moshe Tzvi.

"My prince!" I cried when I opened the door to reveal his pasty face.

"Ah, so it's true what they say about solitary confinement. You've gone insane already."

Just like Rabbi Moritz earlier, Moshe Tzvi arrived with books, even more Talmudic volumes to add to my collection. Moshe Tzvi put them down on the corner of the table.

"What the heck is going on?" I asked him.

Moshe Tzvi looked . . . ill at ease. It was unusual for him. He wasn't usually self-aware enough to express discomfort physically. But he had the look of a person who has a lot to say but doesn't know how to begin.

"Am I in . . . cherem?" I asked him. I figured I was in some kind of exile, but I wasn't sure how official it was.

"Yes," he said, "my understanding is that it is school- and community-wide. I wouldn't expect anybody to speak to you."

"Is that why nobody would talk to me this morning? Chaim? Reuven? They don't want to get seltzered by Rabbi Moritz?"

"No. They don't fear Moritz. But you sinned against them."

"Do you *actually* believe that?" I asked. At this point, it was clear that my dad was biased. He cared more about his own ambitions. And the rabbis weren't who I thought they were. For them, it was more important to control me than to follow their own teachings. But I expected Moshe Tzvi to give it to me straight.

"You should have been there," he said.

They say betrayal is a knife in the back, and that's exactly what Moshe Tzvi's words felt like: they were puncturing, gutting. "For what?" I asked. "So I could get hurt too? So I could have my arm broken? So I could bleed? So I could have my tzitzis torn to shreds?"

"Yes," Moshe Tzvi said solemnly, his head bowed. "I told you I would study for you, and I have. My father and I spent the whole weekend studying for you. Come. Sit."

"*You* sit."

"Very well."

Moshe Tzvi was going full Rabbi Gutman now.

"'Very well'? Don't 'very well' me, you farshtunken asshole."

Moshe Tzvi made like he was going to leave.

"I'm not going to beg you to stay. You *want* to tell me all about your learning. I know you."

"Very well," he said without humor. He sat and opened one of the books. "Hoodie," he began, bringing an official start to our lesson, "let's imagine it's Shabbos. It's Shabbos, and you are walking home from the synagogue. You see a building collapse. Ten people are trapped inside. Nine of them are gentiles, but one of them is me. Do you violate Shabbos, doing the work of pulling me out of the rubble, in order to save our lives?"

"Of course. If your life is at stake, I'm going to do whatever it—"

"Amazing. Now, let's imagine the same scenario. But I'm not in the building. The building contains only gentiles. Do you violate Shabbos to save them?"

"I mean, yeah."

"That's what I would have thought as well. But my father and I studied it, and the Yoma Gemara makes it clear that you are not to violate Shabbos to spare gentiles only."

He showed me the discussion, but I didn't understand enough to contradict his interpretation.

"So I just listen to their cries of horror and anguish, and do nothing?"

"If it makes you feel better, we can imagine that they die quickly and their cries are muffled by the crush of concrete and steel smothering them out of existence."

"Man, I—"

"I know. I wanted to side with you. I wanted to protect you. I tried to find a ruling through which I could exonerate you. I tried so hard. But I'm sorry. It wasn't there. And it's even worse than I thought. Sometimes the text is too clear to contradict. Let us turn to the Avodah Zarah Gemara." Moshe Tzvi opened a second book and leafed through it until he found what he was looking for. "Yes, here it is. I thought of you and that . . . girl, and it was painful to read this. But it is what it is. It is written that you cannot sell large livestock to a gentile, as larger livestock can be used—"

"I'm not planning to sell her large livestock."

"Well, you can't leave them with *small* livestock either, as they are likely to commit—"

"Moshe Tzvi. I don't own so much as a lame ass."

"The message is what matters, Hoodie. The law is clear. They can't be trusted. If a Jewish woman comes from a bath and first encounters a goyishe woman, the Jewish woman must *immediately* return to the bath—think about that. I'm sorry, Hoodie. I don't see any way around it. The rabbis are right. The cherem is just. While your people suffered, you made yourself unclean with a gentile."

I couldn't believe what I was hearing from him. I thought he'd come to rescue me, or to keep me company, or to commiserate with me. That's what your best friend was supposed to do. But he'd come to lecture me, to rub salt in my open wounds. He was just like the rest of them.

I retreated to my window. Moshe Tzvi closed Avodah Zarah and picked up another book. He followed me to the window, holding the book out at me like a weapon.

"I know the rebbe wants you to copy Talmud, but maybe if you return to Tor—"

I couldn't stand him patronizing me. Without thinking, I smacked the book out of his hand. It hit the floor with a thud. I'd figured it was another volume of Talmud, but it was a Chumash, *the* Torah, the most sacred of all books.

We both froze, stock-still, and stared at each other bug-eyed at what I'd just done. Neither of us could believe it.

We stood frozen like that in silence for about thirty seconds. Then Moshe Tzvi bent down, collected the Chumash, kissed it, and put it back on the table. He looked at me once more, with sad droopy eyes, like a puppy. "I'm sorry, Hoodie. I will pray that HaShem forgives you. But as for me . . ."

He didn't finish the sentence. He left and clicked the door closed behind him.

I had the sudden desire to throw another holy book at someone. The problem was that Moshe Tzvi had left the room. I figured I could hit a passerby, but the books were too large and the window too small. I spent the rest of the day in the room, copying Talmud passages I didn't understand. The only good part of the day was lunch, when I realized that Chana had slipped chewing gum into my turkey sandwich. I discovered it too late, and it was both (a) spectacularly disgusting and (b) extraordinarily difficult to separate the turkey and the gum. But I enjoyed the challenge, and I enjoyed picturing Chana's espionage: sneaking into the kitchen under a veil of darkness, hiding individual gum pieces deep in the mustard to avoid their detection.

At home, I expected my house to be volatile, full of hostility. And it was, but I wished the hostility were more open. It was just like school: nobody in the family would talk to me. When I got home that first day of my cherem, Rivkie was playing in the hall between the door and the kitchen. She jumped when I opened the door. She looked all around her for help, for an escape. "It's just me," I said. "It's okay."

Rivkie, little baby Rivkie, shook her head at me, and then ran—literally ran—up the stairs.

And that was the closest interaction I had with any of them, because Rivkie was too young to sense me coming. The rest of them could hear my approach and made themselves immediately scarce. Whenever I came near, they scattered like cockroaches from light.

Within a few hours, I wished somebody would just come in and abuse me. I would have loved my dad to yell at me, or my mom to poke her head out of her bedroom and shoo me like a fly, or Chana to dump soup on my head—Chana was making a concerted transition to liquid projectiles, as they had a wider impact radius.

My father made some aggressive castigatory speeches, but they were directed at his usual target: Tregaron mayor Monica Diaz-O'Leary. She and the council had only hardened their resolve on the zoning laws, and the attack had not had the desired effect on the lawsuit. My dad had hoped that it would cause the town's lawyers to back down, because it would look bad to support people who'd committed a hate crime. But there was no surveillance footage from the crime scene, no proof who'd done it. Diaz-O'Leary wondered out loud—on local TV, in the newspapers—whether the "victims" could have staged the attack themselves for political gain, to make the town appear to have biases it did not.

My father described Diaz-O'Leary and her tactics with an impressive variety of epithets. They appeared in at least four languages, and I'd only heard about half of them before.

Maybe the worst part of my sudden isolation was that I couldn't talk to Anna-Marie. I couldn't tell her that I now knew *exactly* how she felt when nobody would really listen to her. I couldn't tell her that I was there, that I was thinking about her. I wanted to tell her that thinking about her was the only thing keeping me going, that I couldn't sleep at night unless I cleared my mind until she was the only thing in it.

CHAPTER 11

in which there is table moisture, the origin of which is the subject of much speculation

RABBI TAUB CAME TO TOWN on my third day of solitary confinement. My first notebook was full, and Rabbi Moritz had furnished me with a second, bigger one.

Moritz brought me down one level to meet Rabbi Taub.

Rabbi Shneur Yechezkel Taub was like the final boss of rabbis. If you beat him, you won Judaism.

He oversaw the whole community, from Monsey to Brooklyn to Tregaron, and all of its boys' schools. Other than God's own, Rabbi Taub's was the most important voice in our lives. When my father and his company wanted to move a group of us to Tregaron, they had driven up to New York to meet with Rabbi Taub and get his blessing. He had used his personal connections to find us the Presbyterian church and our house.

It only hit me as I was descending the stairs to meet him just how crazy this was: I'd done something so unthinkable that Rabbis Moritz and Friedman didn't know what to do, and they needed a higher authority to come down and make a direct ruling.

Yoel walked me to and from school, and he was the only person who still talked to me. Though I think you could argue that he didn't actually talk *to* me. He talked to himself in my presence. When he found out I was to meet with Rabbi Taub, he was visibly envious. "To meet alone with such a man," he told himself. "What an extraordinary honor that would be."

"If you tongue kiss me in front of the school, we can see him together."

Yoel gave no indication that he'd heard me. Instead, he quoted a famous saying of Rabbi Taub's, then wondered aloud how a mere human could find words full of such brilliance and wisdom.

Rabbi Taub had his own office, the nicest one in the school, even though this was only his second visit to the campus. It was dark in there, but lighter than my prison room. There was a dark wooden desk with gnarled feet, two red leather chairs in front of it. The walls were adorned with photos of famous rabbis and framed diplomas and awards. Behind the desk was another leather chair, but this one was black. The chair was immense and it swallowed up Rabbi Taub, making him appear small and insignificant.

I'd seen pictures of Rabbi Taub—there were two in my

house. But I'd never met him in person. He was very old. I don't even think "old" really does it justice. He was so aged and frail it left you actively wondering how much longer he could possibly live. A few days? A week at the *most*. If I were his family, I'd be on the phone with the market, reserving my bagel and schmear trays for his post-funeral shiva.

Rabbi Moritz left me alone with Rabbi Taub. The old rabbi motioned at one of the red leather chairs and I took a seat. His face was covered in an enormous white beard, and all of his exposed skin was pocked with liver spots. Rabbi Taub smelled like my grandfather but stronger. He smelled like what my grandfather would smell like if you left him out for a while.

You can tell how wise a rabbi is by the percentage of English words he uses. You know Moritz is green because he only tosses in the occasional Hebrew word or phrase. Rabbi Friedman uses more Hebrew and a sprinkling of Yiddish, and you have to concentrate harder to follow him.

I could tell Rabbi Taub was wise as *hell*, because I couldn't understand a word he said. There were more Hebrew words than English ones. I tried my best. I leaned forward over the desk. But all I could pick up was the occasional "the" or "so." He ended most of his incoherent sentences with the phrase, "you see, yes?"

He talked to me for about ten minutes. By that point he was out of breath, and his voice was scratchy. He looked around the desk, searching for something.

"I'll get you some water," I said.

I went out into the hall, down to the teachers' lounge—it was empty—and filled a plastic cup from the sink. I brought it back up and presented it to Rabbi Taub.

"Yasher koach," Rabbi Taub said, thanking me. He took a long drink. Then he stood. It was a great effort. He held on to the edge of the desk for balance. "Nu," he said. "You understand what I've said? You understand what I expect? I know we will all be proud of you one day soon."

I didn't tell him that I'd understood none of what he'd said, and had spent the whole time just hoping that he wouldn't pass away in my presence.

But I found as I went back into the hall that I kind of *had* understood what Rabbi Taub told me, even though I hadn't understood the words themselves. There was something about his vibe, the *way* he spoke that made his meaning clear. Despite the chill of death fast approaching him, he spoke with warmth. His eyes were bright and energetic, and . . . hopeful. He was hopeful for me somehow. He looked at what I'd done, the situation I was in, and instead of a life of painful isolation, he saw some kind of acceptable future for me, one bright enough to put a soft smile on his bearded face.

I didn't see how that future was attainable, but it got the wheels in my head turning, thinking through everything, trying to find a way out of the mess I was in.

I went back into my exile. Rabbi Moritz was waiting for me in my cell. When I came in, he stood watching me expectantly. Eventually it became clear I was supposed to thank him. I did.

"Rabbi Friedman has a softer heart than I," Moritz said. "It was his idea. I hope the meeting was enlightening."

I smiled at him. Moritz thought I was smiling in thanks. But I was smiling because I'd just realized that Rabbi Moritz was jealous of me.

"Do I have to keep copying?" I asked.

"You may transition to self-directed study if you prefer."

"Thank you," I said, pushing a Talmud volume away from me. "I *do* prefer."

That night I couldn't sleep. That was pretty much the usual, except that this time even thinking about Anna-Marie wasn't working.

My mind was full of racing thoughts. They twirled and twisted and writhed in there. But I had no outlet. My family wouldn't look at me. Moshe Tzvi wouldn't speak to me. All of the people I relied on had turned from me, all as punishment for something that didn't even feel wrong.

I wasn't eating much. My usually intense appetite had evaporated like my friendships. But now I went down to the kitchen to see if sustenance could calm me down.

I'd been checking the laptop every night, in case I could use it to get a message out to my unclean girlfriend. I figured if I could make an account on TikTok, I could send her some kind of email thing. But Zippy had taken to using the laptop as a pillow. She slept each night slumped forward on it, her cheek pressed against the Lenovo logo so you could still see it imprinted there in the morning.

It always seemed too risky to pull the computer out from under her. But, you know, desperate times.

I got myself a yogurt and sat across from Zippy, getting her sleeping body used to my presence on the other side of her table/bed. Then I reached out and slowly pulled the laptop toward me. It slid silently across the surface. Zippy's head fell against the wooden tabletop. It made a thud.

I winced.

But she just settled her head onto the table.

I opened the screen and punched in the video app page.

"Did she post anything new?" Zippy mumbled sleepily.

She had posted something new. It was a dance video, shot outside the public high school. I could picture the exact spot—we'd driven by it a hundred times. It was her and that asshole Case. They danced together, in sync with each other. As they danced, they mouthed the lyrics to the song.

My heart was in my throat. I thought I might throw it up onto the table. But I worked to calm down. It was okay, I told myself. They weren't actually dancing *together*. They were dancing next to each other. There was a clear distinction. And they didn't touch or anything.

Had Zippy said something? I looked up over the computer. She was awake now, rubbing her eyes. "Anything good?" she asked.

"How—" I asked. "How—how did you know?"

"You should erase your browser history."

"I don't—like, you can see what I've been looking at?"

"Yep. She's cute. Has a nice smile and a good sense of rhythm."

"Jesus Christ."

"Unfortunately, yes."

We sat in silence for a while. I stared at the wall and listened to the ticking of a clock. I was pretty sure it was a clock, but we didn't own any ticking clocks, and then the ticking got faster and faster, which is un-clocklike. Then I noticed that the table in front of me was soaked. I put an elbow down on the tabletop and my arm started sliding around.

I almost jumped out of my chair. "Why is the table all wet?" I asked Zippy. "Is the roof leaking?"

"We're on the first floor, Hoodie. It's tears, with a decent amount of mucus. You're crying uncontrollably."

"No, I'm not. No chance. I don't cry." I felt my face with my hand. It was undeniably moist. The evidence was stacking up against me.

"Do you want a tissue?"

"No. The table seems to be doing a good job."

We sat there for a bit while I got my weeping under control. "Sister," I said, "you weren't allowed to be with Yoel. I remember—I didn't even understand it at the time—you used to sneak off with him, even though it wasn't allowed. But then . . . nothing happened. At the Wasserstein wedding, I saw you sneak over to the men's side. You were *dancing* with Yoel behind the tent."

"That's different. You're supposed to break that rule. It's expected that you will."

"I don't—"

"A question: Are you allowed to drink alcohol on Purim?"

"I mean, no. It's illegal."

"How many of the students at your yeshiva would you say drink on Purim?"

I laughed and pictured our Purim celebrations. "Every single one of them without exception."

"There are some rules that are supposed to be broken, and some that are not. The problem is that if there is *one* rule you aren't supposed to break, it's the one you're breaking. Think of our orthodoxy like it's surrounded by walls. Break rules inside the walls, fine. But once you go outside the walls to break the rules, then you'll be stuck out there, and you might never get back in." In the low light, I could barely see Zippy's face. But suddenly her voice got more subdued. She sounded a little spacy, a little sad. Her eyes were still on me, but she was looking through me. "There's another thing too," she said. "You're a boy. You're a son. It matters more when you . . . You just . . . You matter more."

"That's not true."

"Of course it's true. It's not always a bad thing. Because I'm a girl, I'm allowed to go straight to college. Nobody's going to be upset that I'm not going for a gap year in Israel. Nobody cares that I'm not in a post–high school study program right now. And even if Yoel weren't Jewish, I could still serve God. My children would still be Jewish, because I'm a woman. If your wife isn't Jewish . . . It's . . . It's unthinkable. What I'm doing isn't what anybody wanted. But in theory there's a balance. I can be an engineer, but I can still get married. I can still have children. I can still follow the commandments. It's not a perfect fit. It's a square peg in a round hole, but with enough WD-40, you can get the square peg in there. There's no square peg, round hole with what you're doing. You're taking the board that contains the hole and setting it on fire. I've been thinking a lot about this, about you."

"Really?"

"Get out of here with your false modesty. You know you're my favorite."

"Can I get that in writing? Maybe you could print, like, a certificate or—"

"I've thought a lot about this. You're standing at the point of no return, on a precipice, looking out on something totally different. If you take that last step, you can still have a great life. But it won't be this one. You have to understand that. It won't be the one you've spent your first fifteen years building toward. It'll be a different life entirely. Who knows? It could be better. But it's final. Once you take that step, you can't turn back. Whoa," Zippy said, as though just realizing the gravity of her own advice. "You're too young to have to make that choice. I'm sorry, kid. It's not fair to you."

"Where is it written that life has to be fair?"

"Nowhere, Hoodie. Nowhere."

"Will you be in that life?" I asked her.

"Not in the same way. Listen, I don't give a rat's you-know-what—"

"Ass."

"Yep. You can date a Muslim boy for all I care. I'm just—if you call me, if you need a place to stay, I'll always be there for you. But it won't be like this. It'll be like in movies where they have to talk across the soundproof glass with old telephones."

I pictured that: me incarcerated, Zippy coming to visit me, me staring at her through the thick glass, us talking through the tinny black telephone on the silver cable.

"You know," I said, "one morning this past summer, I woke up early and saw you praying with Dad's tefillin. I thought I was hallucinating, as one does when one is up before seven. But then I did the same thing the next morning, and you were doing it again. Does Dad know you do that?"

"No."

"Does Yoel know you do that?"

"Yes."

"Does he approve?"

"What if he doesn't? What? He's going to find a new fiancée? Who's got time for that? He knows his place."

I chuckled a little. I should have known better. "Moshe Tzvi says that the law is clear on women—"

"Moshe Tzvi is a maven. He just wants to impress his father. Hopefully he'll grow out of it. Until then, don't listen to him. Jewish law has been up for debate for thousands of years, and it will stay that way. That little putz isn't the final word."

Due to evaporation, my tears were drying up. But they were also drying because I felt a little better. All of the turning gears had done some good—or maybe it was the yogurt. I had an idea forming in my head. A good one, one that might allow me to save myself *and* get me back on the right side of my family, and the community.

I couldn't fight antisemitism with Anna-Marie. I couldn't be part of the community if I was with her, since she wasn't Jewish. But the congregation, the yeshiva, it was my whole life, literally everybody I knew.

Anna-Marie planned to go out into the world and meet all new people, but I always assumed I'd do the opposite. I thought Moshe Tzvi and I would grow up together and compete to see who could have the most outrageous beard, and bounce each other's children on our knees, and rent adjacent cottages on a lake somewhere in the summer so we could collect mosquito bites in unlikely places. It was a clear picture in my mind. Or, it *had* been clear.

Now that Moshe Tzvi wouldn't talk to me, I needed to consider something different. But when I tried to picture an alternate future, I didn't even know what to imagine. It was a void my mind didn't know how to fill.

And I *really* liked Anna-Marie. I felt amazing every time I was with her, every time I *thought* about her. Part of it was physical—she inspired an impressive variety of corporal urges. But it was so much more than that. When we hung out, nobody had an agenda. We were just two people who cared about each other, and that was enough. I didn't like to admit it, even to myself, but it was exactly like what Zippy said about Yoel:

When I was alone with Anna-Marie, I felt whole. I couldn't just let that feeling go. I wasn't going to let anybody take that feeling away from me.

It seemed like a problem with no solution. But now I saw the solution, one that would let me stay with Anna-Marie, and might even bring me back from exile. And it was so clear that I wondered how I could possibly not have seen it before.

If the peg is square, you get one of those lathe machines, and you round that thing.

CHAPTER 12

in which I put my metaphorical lathe to use

"IT'S A BEAUTIFUL DAY," I said to Yoel at the curb.

"It's raining," Yoel observed.

"You say 'potato.' I say 'potahto.'"

"Nobody says 'potahto,' Hoodie. Let's get moving."

Yoel was never in a hurry, but since he couldn't read in the rain, he wanted to get me to school as soon as possible.

That morning I didn't even complain when, after Shacharis, Rabbi Moritz accompanied me upstairs. It took him aback when I dove right into the Talmud. I asked him if I could have a dictionary, or a Moshe Tzvi, to help me understand what I was reading. He brought me a Talmud-specific dictionary to help me decipher the combination of old Hebrew and Aramaic.

I was copying from the Sanhedrin Gemara. The goal of copying this particular passage was to get me to appreciate the significance of Jewish life. It said that if one Jewish life is saved, it is as though the whole world were saved.

I worked more slowly than usual, because, for once, I was actually reading, tracing my fingers slowly over the letters, cross-referencing with my dictionary. By the time Mincha came around, I felt like I was starting to understand a little of what Moshe Tzvi was always yammering on about. When you could actually understand it, reading Talmud was like talking to very old rabbis. It was like talking to Rabbi Taub, if he were a thousand years older.

After Mincha, Rabbi Moritz came to accompany me back upstairs, but I put the first part of my peg-shaving plan in motion. "Rebbe," I said, "since the rain has stopped, I was hoping to take you up on the tree walk rain check."

He was nonplussed.

"I was to show you my favorite neighborhood trees. I have a lot on my mind from the Sanhedrin Gemara, and I thought I could process it better if I took a walk with an arbor-appreciative focus."

"Right," he said. "Fine. I have class. But would you like to take the walk yourself? I'll meet you in my office in an hour. I can experience the arboriculture vicariously."

"Fine," I said. "Very well." I nodded to him and started my stroll.

Anna-Marie's school had just let out, and I didn't think she'd be home for a bit. So I walked around the block in circles, practicing what I was going to say. In each loop, I stopped at our tree and touched it for good luck. When I felt that enough time had passed, I walked to her house.

I rang the doorbell. It felt creepy to peer inside through the small pane of glass on the door, so I stood with my back to the door, facing the street. The sun was starting to poke through the clouds. It was humid from the rain, but there was a steady breeze that rustled the leaves, which were starting to turn.

When nobody answered the doorbell, I knocked. And this time I did peer inside. I couldn't see anybody but I could hear two voices. The voices were elevated. The inhabitants were yelling at each other, but their voices were muffled by a couple of walls, and by the door itself. I couldn't pick out any words.

I was about to give up on the whole thing when the door opened about a foot. A reddened, flushed mayor looked out at me. She tried to compose herself quickly. "Ye-hoo-dee. I—was Anna-Marie expecting you?"

"I doubt it," I said. "Can I come in? I can't be seen out—" I decided not to finish that sentence, but I kept my head on a swivel, looking up and down the street.

"Um. Hold on a minute, sweetie."

Anna-Marie replaced her mother at the door. She had the same look, her cheeks and eyes red. "What're you doing here?" she asked. She looked annoyed, but I hoped the annoyance was for her mother. "I texted you a hundred times. I thought something was *wrong*. Then I thought you ghosted me, and now you just show up at my—"

I couldn't stand in the open any longer. "I'm sorry for this,"

I said. I pushed my way inside and closed the door behind me. "And I'm sorry I didn't reply. I couldn't. I lost my phone."

"Did you try calling it?"

"It was confiscated."

"For what?"

"I'll get there. Can we talk?"

"Why don't we go for a walk? I want to get out of here."

"I can't. I—I can't be seen with you."

Monica Diaz-O'Leary was sitting at the kitchen table. You could see straight through from the foyer. She was watching us but trying to make it look like she wasn't. Anna-Marie looked at her mom, then back at me. "Okay," she said.

Anna-Marie went straight up the stairs toward her bedroom. I followed.

She sat on the edge of her bed. This time I took the leap across the threshold and sat in the plastic office chair at her desk. The room smelled like her, like detergent with a hint of something floral. It filled my whole head, made my thoughts foggy. I tried to clear the fog. I needed to concentrate on what I was going to say.

But Anna-Marie went first. "What did you lose your phone for? Anything good?"

"Yeah," I said. "Pretty good." Because Anna-Marie was pretty good. In all of this awful crap, she was the one good thing. "I saw your latest video thing, the dance with that kid Case. He's a jerk, but that dance was sick."

Anna-Marie looked surprised, but not in a good way. Her

mouth was frozen half-open. She squinted her eyes at me. "You were *watching* my videos?"

"Yeah."

"That's . . . weird."

I didn't get it. "Why? Isn't that the point? Isn't it on there to be seen?"

"No. It's not . . . public. I mean, it's public, but social media . . . It's weird if somebody's just *watching* you. It's like you have a stalker. It's different if *you* also post, and then I would see yours, and you would see mine, and we could comment and stuff. But—I don't know—it's different."

I still didn't understand. Why would you post a video you didn't want somebody to see? It made no sense.

"I'm sorry," I said. "I didn't know, like, the rules."

"It's okay," she said. But it didn't seem okay. She shrank away from me, moving from the edge of her bed to the pillow side.

I needed to get her back. "So," I said, "I got my phone taken because I was talking to you. I can't be with somebody who's not Jewish. When I was with you the other night and all that stuff happened, I got in trouble because I was with you, not with my friends."

"That's crazy. If you were with them, you would have—"

"I know, I know. Still. They see it as a betrayal, like I'm turning away from my people."

"By hanging out with somebody else? That's . . . intense."

"Yeah. 'Intense' is the right word."

Anna-Marie produced a wry laugh, a laugh without humor. "I thought *my* mom was demanding."

"Well, so," I started to say. I wanted to get up and pace around. If I was going to make a speech, I felt like I needed to be on my feet.

I went for it. I stood up and walked into the middle of the room like I was about to deliver a monologue in a play. "Are you still going to NYU?"

"If I get in, yeah."

"I was doing some research, and Yeshiva University is pretty close to NYU. They're both in Manhattan. So I thought of a solution. After we graduate, we could move to New York together. It would work, so long as we got engaged, and you agreed to convert to Judaism—you wouldn't have to actually convert now. You'd just have to *agree* to do it when we got married. Then we—"

Anna-Marie's eyes were wide, and she was leaning forward toward me like she was trying to hear better. "Did you just say *marry* you?"

"Yeah. But not now. We could get married after high school, or even after college. You would have to agree to convert beforehand, though. Then I wouldn't be breaking halachic—"

"Oh my God, Hoodie. Are you actually—what is wrong with you?"

Anna-Marie was laughing, but again it wasn't a real laugh.

I didn't expect her to immediately agree. But I expected her to listen, to think about it, to see the sense in the idea.

"Do you hear what you're saying? *Marry* you? I'm *fifteen*. What am I, some kind of child bride? That's some backward crap, man. I thought my mom was just being herself when she said you guys live in the past."

"We wouldn't get married *now*. I already said that. It's just an agreement to—"

"Go back to Babylon, dude." Now she was laughing for real. Laughing at me. I wished I wasn't standing in the middle of the room. "Go back to wandering the desert. Go invent the wheel. You can move things around with very little friction. It's cool. You'll see."

"No, listen," I said. *"Please."* I was getting desperate. This had to work. I cared too much about her. I couldn't lose her. I'd already lost everybody else. "I've thought it through. I'm not saying it's perfect. But I don't see any other way we can continue to be together."

She stopped laughing, her smile instantly erased. Her voice grew quiet. "Be together?" she asked.

"Yeah," I said.

She shook her head a single time. "What do you mean? No. We're not *together*."

Now it was my turn to be confused. I didn't understand what she was saying. Of course we were together. We were *literally* together. I was in *her room*. "What?" I said. I started pacing back and forth. "What are *you* talking about? You touched me. You touched me on the arm. You *hugged* me. You pressed your body against mine. The body is sacred, protected by God. You don't just stick yours against somebody else's if you don't—"

165

Anna-Marie had her hand over her face. I wanted to make eye contact with her but couldn't.

"You don't even know anything about me," she said.

"Yeah, I—"

"What's my favorite color? What's my favorite song? What's my biggest fear?"

I didn't know the answer to any of those questions. "Your room is very green," I noted.

"We're friends, at the *most*," she said. "I find you interesting."

I could feel a buried anger growing in me, rising to the surface. It took over my body to the point where I could feel it in my fingers like a kind of electricity. "You find me *interesting*? Am I like something in a museum, behind a display case? So, what? Now that you've looked at me and read my little plaque, you can move on to the next exhibit?"

"No. It's not like that at all. I do like you. We're just . . . We live in different worlds, Hoodie."

"We live in the same world. There's only one world. *You* said that to me."

"No, there isn't. Don't call them 'worlds' if you don't want to. But you . . . You're like a time traveler in a sci-fi movie. You've come here to visit, but eventually you have to go back to your own time, you know?"

"No. Sometimes in those movies the time traveler stays, because he falls in love with—" I cut myself off there, but it was too late.

"Don't say that," Anna-Marie said. She shrank deeper into

her corner, pressed her forehead against the wall. "Jesus. I can't believe this is happening. This just can't be happening right now. I can't deal with this. This isn't real." Anna-Marie's voice rose as she talked. She was angry, her voice choked. "I only—I *only* hung out with you in the first place because my *mom* wanted me to. She thought she would look better in the town, in the stupid news, if I was seen hanging out with a Jewish guy. When we erased the graffiti on the gravestones, that was my mom's idea. She didn't want anybody to know that stuff was there, and she thought it would be good for her if I walked around with you. And now you think I'm your *girlfriend*? You think I'm going to agree to move to *New York* with you? You think you *love* me? This isn't love. This isn't how love works. But what would you know about anything real? We haven't even kissed or—"

"I'll kiss you," I said. I took a step toward her bed, but she shrank even farther away, pressing herself into the corner where the two walls met.

"Do you know how anything actually works in the real world? I doubt it. You live your life by a book some drunk dudes wrote thousands of years ago."

I would argue that, at that moment, a hole simply appeared in her wall. But I have to admit that the evidence suggested otherwise. There was the throbbing of my hand, for example, and the little bits of plaster and paint stuck between my knuckles.

My whole body was numb except for my hand, which pulsed. As I processed the sudden pain, I tried to process her words.

It had all been a lie.

She'd used me.

I thought the growing anguish would tear me apart, like I would physically break into pieces, ripped at the seams.

The door to the bedroom burst open, and the mayor appeared looking panicked. "Baby, are you okay?" she said, looking at Anna-Marie.

"Get *out* of here, Mom," Anna-Marie shouted. I'd never heard her shout before. "This is *your* fault."

Mrs. Diaz-O'Leary didn't respond to her daughter. She turned to me instead. "Young man, you need to leave this house right now."

I shook some plaster off my hand and turned to leave. I took one last look at Anna-Marie. She was curled up in the corner of her bed, staring down at her pillow. "I gave up everything for you," I said.

"*Now*," the mayor growled.

"Why?" Anna-Marie asked her pillow. "Why would you do that?" Her anger had given way to pity. She felt bad for me, and her pity hurt even more than her fury.

Why? I asked myself the same question. Why? Because she was an amazing, beautiful, special person? Because I was an idiot, the exact know-nothing she said I was? I didn't want to say either of those things. So I said nothing. I walked past the mayor, down the stairs, and out into the street.

CHAPTER 13

in which an unknown party takes a famous photo of me

HAVE YOU EVER WANTED TO bury yourself alive? Get a shovel? Dig a sizable hole? Fall face-first into it, and just wait for everything to fade to black? I was all ready to do it. I think the only shovel we owned was a snow shovel, but the ground was soft from the rain, so it might have worked. The main problem was that once you were lying down in the grave you'd dug yourself, you needed somebody to fill it in for you. I couldn't think of a single person in the world who cared enough about me just then to do me that favor.

I forgot all about my appointment with Rabbi Moritz. I forgot all about school. I more or less forgot where I was. I was just walking, wandering. I was a kind of worn, delirious mess. I found I was walking quickly, swiftly, like I had a destination I was in a hurry to reach. Maybe I was looking for a ready-made hole in the ground.

I just wanted to be lying down, somewhere dark, somewhere I could be unconscious, somewhere I could not feel. I was in too much pain to be awake to feel it. Did they make Novocain for your entire body?

I walked for a long time, paying no attention to where I was going. After a while, I found myself walking along the commuter rail tracks. There was trash all over the ground, litter of potato chip bags and beer cans. At the top of the ridge near the station, I could see down into the cemetery. There were police lights spinning around in the graveyard, and I could hear distant shouting. But I didn't think anything of it.

On the other side of the tracks, I had a view of the dirt lot where the apartment building was supposed to be. I could see my dad's office trailer. He was probably in there right then with the shades drawn, doing paperwork with the light from his cheap desk lamp. The excavator still sat idle, in the same place it had sat for weeks.

I cut through the trees and walked across the lot. I'd seen the digital plans for the building. I was walking through what was supposed to be the first floor, with the gym, the lobby, the communal spittoon. I walked through the imaginary double doors at the front of the building and onto the sidewalk.

I was only a block from the main strip of town. I thought maybe if I got a snack, the taste of said snack could distract me from all of the other unpleasant sensations.

It was late afternoon—between 4:22 and 4:24—when I jingled my way into the Abramowitz market. At about the same time, a U-Haul pulled up at the curb. I waited to see if somebody would get out of the van, in case they needed me to hold the door for them. But it just idled there, and I went inside.

I was thinking I'd grab some Starburst, but for once I wasn't in the mood—they reminded me too much of Anna-Marie. I went two aisles over where the chips, crackers, and popcorn were located.

Mr. Abramowitz stood behind the register, reading something on his phone. He had looked up and frowned when I came in. It could have been because I was me, the apikores. But maybe it was just because I was supposed to be in school.

I was never in the market at this time of day, during school. I was always there when it was filled with kids grabbing snacks, shouting greetings and jokes across the store, chasing each other around.

The market was fairly busy now—it was the only kosher store in town—but it was more subdued. It was mostly women shopping for dinner. Mrs. Gutman and her oldest daughter were at the deli counter waiting for service from Elad, the guy who helped Mr. Abramowitz before Chaim got out of school.

Two of Zippy's friends, Esther and Avigail, were standing in front of the dairy coolers. They were holding baskets, but both baskets were empty. Avigail leaned on one of the refrigerator handles. They looked like they'd been there awhile, just chatting.

Mrs. Goldberg was one aisle over from me. She was

checking the expiration dates on jars of herring, picking them off the shelf one by one, holding them up by her nose, turning them, placing them back on the shelf. None of them was to her liking. She snorted at the herring in disgust and moved on to the gefilte fish.

I turned away from Mrs. Goldberg and looked over the potato chip options. There were many enticing possibilities. I decided on an onion flavor I'd never tried before—onion is a vegetable, so they'd be good for me. I put my hand on the bag, but then I noticed somebody at the corner of my vision. It was Anna-Marie. She was reaching for a pack of Starburst. She looked as miserable as I felt, her face pale but splotchy with red, her eyes downcast. In case she decided to cast her eyes upward, I ducked down so she wouldn't see me, which is why I'm still alive.

Because as soon as I crouched down, I heard the first shot. Even before I heard the sound itself, the bag of chips I'd been reaching for exploded. The chips flew in all directions, and started raining down, but I couldn't tell what was chip and what wasn't because lots of other stuff was flying around: glass, food, blood.

I wondered later why I hadn't heard them enter the store. But it's because they didn't use the door. The same shot that killed my chips shattered one of the panes of glass that separated the market from the street. They came in through the space where the window used to be.

I sat crouched down on the linoleum floor. I put my hand to my head and knocked off my Borsalino. I could still feel my kippah there, so I left the hat on the floor.

On one side of my aisle were boxes of crackers, on the other, bags of chips. There were little specks of blood on the top row of chip bags, but I didn't know whose blood it was.

My mind went blank, wiped clean, like a piece of fresh printer paper. My body went blank too, like it wasn't a body at all, just an unincorporated mix of muscle and bone, like the model of a body a teacher would use in a classroom.

I'd never heard a gun in real life before. It was louder than I expected. Maybe that's why I couldn't think: all the noise. As the shots rang out, they sounded like they were firing inside my head, reverberating through my body. Between shots, my ears rang with pulsating tones, like two notes slightly out of tune with each other.

There must have been other sounds too. People scream as they are hunted and shot. But I didn't hear any of those sounds. I just heard the shots, hoping that I would keep hearing them, because when you're dead you stop hearing things.

I saw them when I looked up the aisle toward the street. The front window of the store was split up into four large panes. The first one had been shot through, but the other three were still intact. I could see their reflections in the glass.

Two people, wearing bulletproof vests and tactical belts. One carried a large assault rifle. It was black. It looked heavy. He had the butt of the rifle pressed against his chest, the barrel pointed outward. In the reflection I could see it flash when he pulled the trigger. The other shooter, a woman, had a smaller gun. It looked kind of like a pistol, but it had a long magazine hanging down below it. If Moshe Tzvi had been there, he could have told me what kind of gun it was. But I was glad Moshe Tzvi wasn't there.

I got even lower down on the floor, into the prone position, and began to shimmy along the floor toward the window. I should have tried to sneak out the back through the storeroom, but my blank mind didn't consider that. It just saw the outside world through the window and wanted to go there.

I could see in the reflection that the shooters were near the front of the store, facing the counter. So when I got to the end of the aisle, I got up off the floor. I half-stood, half-crouched, unsure what to do.

I'd always thought of a gun as a process. Somebody holds the gun. That person pulls the trigger. Some kind of science happens in the gun, and it shoots a little metal cylinder out of the barrel. The bullet travels through the air, and embeds itself in its target, except when the target is very soft and/or thin, in which case it passes through the target until it meets something more substantial.

But there isn't a process with a gun. It is instantaneous, like magic. The hole appears at the same moment the trigger is pressed—in the market it almost seemed like the hole preceded the trigger pull.

Here's what a gun is: a gun is a long-distance hole punch. Here it made a hole in the wall. There it made a hole in Mr. Abramowitz's neck. Here it made a hole in Elad's stomach as he came over the counter, reaching out toward the first shooter's weapon. There it made a hole in a grape juice bottle. The Kedem spilled onto the floor, where it pooled with Elad's blood.

I stood stock-still, watching purple blend with red. I was frozen there until somebody crashed into me and knocked me to the floor.

It was Anna-Marie. She'd made a run for it, bursting out of her aisle. But I'd been in her way. She'd bowled me over like a linebacker and now we were in a heap on the linoleum, a pile of mixed-up limbs and tzitzis.

We both scrambled up as quickly as we could. I eyed the door, but it was too far away, too close to where the shooters were standing. They were up near the counter, but they were just now turning toward the rest of the store.

I looked at the glass. I didn't understand how it was still intact. There were holes in everything. Shot after shot rang out.

There was a display rack that held bananas. They were on sale. I grabbed the rack and swung it at the window. It made a kind of clang, and the banana bunches flew all over. The glass shook but remained intact. I swung again. This time the window shattered, but not in the way I expected. I was hoping the glass would shatter completely, into a million tiny pieces, leaving nothing but air in the space between the market and the sidewalk. But instead, it broke into just a few pieces. The banana rack went through the window, and bounced around on the sidewalk. It left a jagged hole in the window, large enough for a person to slip through, but it had little shards sticking inward, like sharp teeth in a mouth of glass.

I was closer to the window, but I grabbed Anna-Marie and shoved her toward it. She got stuck partway through, with her head and arms outside, but the rest of her in the store.

Over the din of the gunshots, the second shooter had noticed the window breaking. She turned her gun on me, and I felt the hole appear in my chest. In the split second immediately following the shot, I remember thinking: The chest. Huh. Are there any important organs in the chest?

But then I turned back to Anna-Marie and the window. I reached to help her through the window, but the second bullet hit me in the back of my left arm, just below the shoulder. So I used my foot instead. I kicked at Anna-Marie, pummeling her through the opening in the glass. She tumbled out of the store, and I followed, diving out onto the sidewalk.

When the bullets had hit me, I'd felt them, in the sense that I *knew* I'd been shot. But the pain didn't hit until I was outside. I remember that moment vividly, on my hands and knees on the sidewalk, looking at my own blood on the concrete. I had no idea how much blood the human body contained, but I was disturbed at how much of mine had left my body in favor of the sidewalk.

The next thing I felt was Anna-Marie. She grabbed my right hand and started pulling me up. When I couldn't stand at first, she slipped her other arm under my left shoulder and pulled me to my feet. She's a slight person. She had gashes all up and down her legs. I don't know how she managed it.

We started running. Well, not *running*. Hobbling, but

hobbling fast, up the sidewalk away from the store, our arms wrapped around each other. In the most famous of the photos, the one where the ambulance is just pulling up, you can see us standing there, leaning on each other, our arms intertwined, my head pressed against hers, a single trail of blood behind us on the pavement, like the tail of some kind of messed-up comet.

The police cars arrived just as Anna-Marie was dragging me to my feet. They came from both directions, screeching to a halt, emptying officers into the street.

As we hobble-ran up the block, the sounds escalated. What had been a steady drumbeat of shots became a frenzy. It was like that moment in the popcorn-popping process where it really gets going, where the single pops become so frequent that they blend together into one solid wall of popcorn sound.

An ambulance screamed around the corner. It was definitely heading for the store, but the driver saw us and slammed on the brakes. Ambulance people—one of them was named Tracy—spilled out of the vehicle, and rushed toward us. They separated Anna-Marie and me and hustled us into the back of the ambulance.

They asked questions. Anna-Marie answered. This is how they learned that I was shot, but she wasn't. So I got the stretcher. She sat on the side, on a little bench.

In movies, when somebody gets shot, they usually just pass out, and then they either live or they don't. The movie cuts to the next scene, where they're recovering in a hospital bed, or getting lowered into a grave surrounded by their grieving family.

I wish it actually worked that way, because I remember *so* much about the ambulance ride.

I remember Tracy telling me that everything was fine and that I would be all right. I remember telling Tracy that everything was *not* all right: I was shot. Twice. Had *she* ever been shot twice? If *she'd* been shot twice, she wouldn't be telling me everything was all hunky-dory. But I'm not sure if my words came out as words. She got an oxygen mask on me pretty quick.

I remember Anna-Marie hyperventilating, taking rapid shallow breaths, saying, "Oh my God, Hoodie. Oh my God, Hoodie. Oh my God. Hoodie, are you—oh my God."

I remember that when I wasn't moaning incoherently or abusing Tracy, I was praying vigorously. I made a lot of promises. I promised God that if he saved me, I would never betray him again. I would never turn away from him or his Torah. I promised the same things to my parents. I promised Leah I would never leave the toilet seat up. I promised Zippy that my aim would be true or I'd clean the bathroom floor myself. I promised Chana that I'd always open the window in the bathroom so that it wouldn't smell when I—I'm not sure why all my promises were bathroom related.

The part that sticks with me, that will always be with me, that I experience every night in my dreams, and comes to me unexpectedly during the day—other than the excruciating pain and the mortal fear—is the sound of the ambulance siren. We always hear ambulances coming or going, and their movement warps our experience of the sound. It gets higher as it approaches, lower as it moves away. But *in* the ambulance, every wail of the siren is the same eerie, chilling pitch.

I don't remember much after we got to the hospital. I have a vague recollection of the part when they wheeled me off the ambulance into the building. But then I was in surgery, and I remember none of that.

The second bullet had gone straight through my arm. They didn't need to remove it from my body, because it was still back in downtown Tregaron, probably in a wall across the street from the market, based on the trajectory. It had torn through my skin, and my biceps, but that was all.

The first bullet was in my upper chest. It had shattered my clavicle, which, according to the doctor, is a bone. The bullet had hit me high enough to miss my internal organs, but low enough to miss the arteries in my neck. The doctor told me I should "thank my lucky stars" for that. Instead I thanked God, and the doctor herself. She'd closed the wound before I'd lost a fatal amount of blood. I didn't ask her how close I'd been to that point. But, later, Chana did. The doctor said, "Maybe you'll learn someday when you become a hospital doctor, little lady."

Chana informed the doctor that she planned to be the person putting people *in* the hospital, not the one saving them once they were there.

The doctor was horrified, obviously. She left the room.

I laughed, then winced in pain, and the nurse scolded me for laughing, as though I could do anything about it.

The doctor said I would recover more or less fully, but

there was a decent chance I'd never have the same mobility in my left shoulder. The healing and rehab would be long and painful.

I thought to myself that Chaim would probably be the best shooter on the JV team once again. But I never found out if he fully recovered from his arm fractures. His father was killed in the shooting, and right after the shiva they moved to Lakewood to be with his mother's family.

CHAPTER 14

*in which my father throws things at me,
and I throw Rivkie at things*

IT WAS IMPOSSIBLE FOR MY family to shelter me from any of the aftermath. It was all over the news, on every channel. I could watch it on the little TV that hung up in the corner of the hospital room.

The shooting had left four people dead, not counting the perpetrators. Mr. Aryeh Abramowitz, Mr. Elad Parra, and Mrs. Freida Goldberg were shot and killed in the market. Officer David Ryan had been shot and killed in the cemetery *before* the shooting at the market—it was his patrol car lights I'd seen from the train tracks. I have to tell myself that God granted all four of them eternal life in the next world.

After a long shoot-out, both attackers were killed by police.

Surveillance footage of the shooting leaked online. Thousands of people watched it before moderators were able to take it down. The video has resurfaced a few times on YouTube, but usually only for a few minutes. Moshe Tzvi watched it. He said that "[I] took those bullets like a total badass, bro," but I haven't watched it. I won't watch it. I already have to relive it in my dreams for the rest of my life.

I have to wake up in the middle of the night with imaginary gunshots ringing in my ears. And sometimes, when I close my eyes, I see the look Elad had on his face when the first bullet entered his abdomen, and I have to stop whatever I'm doing and gather myself. And often, when I lie in bed at night I want to just scream, to call out, because I'm not sure if I screamed at the time, and for some reason it feels important to know either way, but I never will. I asked Anna-Marie, but she doesn't know, and she's not as comfortable talking about it as I am. When I bring it up, she gets this distant look on her face, and disappears into herself.

The shooters had been radicalized into an antisemitic religious group. They hated Jews. Their social media pages were filled with hate messages and anti-Jewish memes. They'd read about Tregaron on the news, how the Jews were invading, taking over the town, staging antisemitic violence to manipulate the media narrative in their favor, as those crafty Jews are wont to do. So they decided that if Monica Diaz-O'Leary wasn't going to do anything about it, they would do it themselves.

First, they drove their stolen U-Haul to the cemetery, but it's unclear why—the Jews there were already dead. I guess they could have been the ones who did the original graffiti, but we'll never know.

Officer David Ryan happened to be at the cemetery, meeting an informant. When he noticed the shooters' stolen van, he confronted them. They shot and killed him.

Then the shooters drove to the Abramowitz Family Kosher Market, where they got out of the van and opened fire. Two victims escaped. Three victims were killed. The rest were trapped inside while the police and the attackers exchanged fire for almost an hour. Avigail Zilber was injured, but she received treatment after the shoot-out, and survived.

After the firefight, investigators found a long handwritten note in the U-Haul. The manifesto explained how the shooters were helping preserve the purity of the human race by exterminating Jews. It said that since Jews were the enemy of God, they were also the enemy of the shooters, and of everybody else.

The investigators also found a pipe bomb in the van. They weren't sure what the attackers had planned to use it for, but when they unlocked the first shooter's phone, they saw that he had searched for the address of the yeshiva, so our school might have been the next target.

Most of the fact-finding part of the news cycle happened while I was still in the ICU, hooked up to various tubes. I don't remember much of that. I was cold. There were lots of whirrs and beeps. I caught up on it all when I was in recovery.

There were a lot of "narratives" on the TV news. People talked about the rise of hate crimes, and the need to deradicalize extremists. People talked about how the country needed to do better at identifying people with mental health problems, and get them the services they required. People talked about how there shouldn't be as many guns, because guns are designed to kill people. Other people talked about how there should be more guns, because if Mrs. Goldberg had had a gun in her purse, she could have wasted these maniacs the second they blasted their way into the store.

But there was also the narrative that made me famous, at least for a little while.

The surveillance video wasn't the only recording of the shooting. On the main business strip in Tregaron, the first floors of the buildings were all businesses: shops and restaurants. The second and third floors were all apartments. Somebody across the street from the market had taken a video of the shooting through their apartment window.

When Anna-Marie and I were huddled together, hobbling up the block, that person had zoomed in on us. Somebody had turned the video into still photos. There was one photo in particular that ended up everywhere: the home page of every news website, the front page of every newspaper, the graphic that hovered on the screen while commentators argued on TV.

The picture shows an Orthodox Jewish teenager. He's wearing a dark suit, but where the jacket hangs off his shoulder, you can see that his tzitzis and white button-up shirt are soaked in blood. His eyes are shut, his face distorted in pain. His arms cling to a girl. She's wearing a short-sleeve T-shirt, but it's scrunched up, exposing her stomach. Her shirt and skin are streaked with blood. She's wearing jean shorts, and her legs are sliced up, deep red gashes on all sides. Her eyes are wide with terror. Between them the two kids are wearing three shoes. They have their arms wrapped around each other in a kind of symbiotic way, like neither of them can stand without the other. Their cheeks are pressed together, his wispy mustache against the side of her nose.

Only two people who saw the photo knew the full story, that he was in love with her, that she had just rejected his love, that in his despair he'd gone to get potato chips. That she had been angry at him for being so naive and at her mother for being so controlling, that in her anger she had gone to get some British Starburst. They'd driven each other to the store, then saved each other's lives there.

Only Anna-Marie and I knew the full story, but the photo still became a kind of symbol. People used it to suggest that our divisions were shallow, that we could all get along after all. People talked about Anna-Marie and me like we'd staged the photo to encourage people to get along with each other, like we'd paused in our communal bleeding to pose for a photo op. One pundit described the shot as a "blurry portrait of the universal humanity to which hate and violence reduces us."

When Anna-Marie and I are super old, I plan to text her every so often and say, "Hey, remember when hate and violence reduced us to universal humanity?"

To which she'll reply, "Yes, President Rosen, I do recall."

I spent four fully conscious days in the hospital. In a strange, messed-up way, they were good days. I hadn't processed the tragedy yet, that four people were dead. I didn't yet feel guilty that I'd survived while others hadn't. I hadn't begun the journey of working through the trauma, figuring out how to live with it on a daily basis. I just knew I was alive, and people were talking to me again.

Each of those days was like the best of Shabbos. The hospital food wasn't kosher, so I got all kinds of amazing stuff from the outside world: my mom's roast chicken, spaghetti and meatballs, General Tso's chicken from the kosher Chinese restaurant in Colwyn.

My family packed the hospital room and spilled out into the hallway. The nurses loved us—that's sarcastic. We were numerous and rowdy, and you could tell we annoyed the hell out of them, with the girls climbing all over the hospital bed, the chairs, the windowsill, running up and down the hall. They kept telling my parents that the girls were running around, like my parents didn't know, like my parents could or would do something about it.

Just like Shabbos, we played a lot of board games. We laid the boards out on the floor, and somebody would play as my proxy, rolling the dice for me, moving my pieces.

Lots of community members came to visit. People brought flowers. Rabbi Friedman came. So did Rabbi Moritz. It was nice to have my people around me again, but I felt like their acceptance should have come with an apology. It didn't, of course. It wouldn't. And I'd just have to be okay with that.

And it wasn't everybody. There were lots of people who were conspicuously absent. The Gutmans never came. Every time the door opened, I expected—I hoped—Moshe Tzvi would walk through. But my supposed best friend didn't visit me once.

In the evening, the third night, most of the family had gone home. Zippy was sitting with me at the side of the bed. Leah was asleep in the other chair. Zippy and I were just chatting.

"How was the pork?" she asked me.

I didn't recall eating any.

"The nurses told me you had some. They didn't know about it. They had stripped your clothes." I must have looked scared, because Zippy said, "Come on, you know it's okay. If you're starving alone in the forest, and a pig comes along, you have to eat the pig."

"How am I going to eat the pig, Zippy? Is it just going to present itself to me for slaughter? I'm weak. I'm starving."

"You know what I'm saying."

My father came in, walking briskly.

"Abba, have you ever had pork?" Zippy asked him.

He paused in the center of the room. "Once. A gentile boy in school sprinkled bacon bits on my salad. When I fought him, *I* was the one they suspended. That's when I decided I would do whatever I could to ensure that *my* children got a *Jewish* education."

He went to the corner to rouse Leah. As he passed the bed, he tossed me a newspaper. He'd circled a front-page article with a Sharpie. He did this at least once per day: walked in and delivered me Jewish news, throwing a paper onto the bed like a paper boy in an old TV show.

It was hard to tell how forgiving my father was.

The very first moment they were allowed in my room, my parents burst through the door and rushed to the bed. They hugged me in an overwhelming, aggressive, almost violent way. It hurt in my shoulder, and also at the base of my throat where I could feel tears coming on.

After the hug, my father stood at my bedside, red-eyed, smiling through silent tears. Zippy insists he was smiling because I was still alive, and I believe her. But I also think he was smiling because of the situation with the lawsuit and the high-rise.

While I was in the ICU, my father and his company were calling reporters and journalists, telling them all about the lawsuit between them and the city of Tregaron, about how the town wouldn't let the Jews build an apartment building.

To avoid the bad publicity, the mayor and town council held an emergency meeting and reversed their decision. They didn't have a choice. It would look too bad if they still stonewalled the project.

It had taken a shooting of his people to make it happen, but my father had finally won. Construction would begin. The idled construction equipment would be idle no more.

He was thrilled. You could tell he knew he should hide it—people he cared about were dead, and he certainly mourned their losses. But there was a part of him that couldn't help but revel in his victory. In his mind, his was the story of the Jewish people: First you faced persecution. Then the persecution led to violence. Finally, if you were persistent, if you were smart, if you had strength, you got to build your high-rise with its nonporous countertops and shiny new spittoons. In his mind, he embodied the resolute nature of his people. You could see it in the way he carried himself. Even in my hospital room, he had his chest puffed out, strutting like a rooster.

The article he'd circled this time was by a prominent Israeli rabbi. It said that the media narrative surrounding "the photo" was misguided. Antisemitic violence did not excuse the lack of tznius on the part of the girl. Sure, it was acceptable for the wounded Jew to lean on her in that moment, but that did not excuse the prior relationship he had with her, which clearly violated Jewish law. The rabbi wished me well, but could not keep from placing some of the blame for the violence on me—I'd invited this kind of thing by crossing a sacred line.

My father wouldn't say it to me. He was letting the newspaper tell me. But some people weren't going to forgive me. That's why some of our community wouldn't come to the hospital. They would always blame me in a way. They would always believe that my actions had contributed to the tragedy. They would think of Mr. Abramowitz and Mrs. Goldberg and Elad and believe that, if not for me, they'd still be alive. Maybe my father was one of those people. He wouldn't say.

Either way, I needed him to know how I felt. My perspective was just as valid as his, and if he didn't recognize that, we were going to have a lot of trouble living in the same house for the next couple years.

I would have preferred to just talk it out, like adults, but since my dad insisted on this passive-aggressive system, I started circling the articles that defended me, and passing the papers back to him the next day. I wasn't sure if he actually read the articles I circled, but he always received the paper with a nod, and tucked it under his arm.

That day, as my dad and Leah were moving to leave, I opened the newspaper to his circled article. I pretended to read it for the three seconds it took them to get out of the room.

I could hear their footsteps head down the hall, but then they stopped, and suddenly they were back in the room. My dad looked like he'd seen a ghost.

Which he had. Or, the closest thing anyway.

Because Rabbi Taub stood in the doorway. "Stood" is not really the right word. He was in the doorway, but whether or not he was standing was up for interpretation. He was so stooped that his eyes faced straight down at the ground. If he'd bent down any farther, his long beard would have touched the floor. He put his skeletal hand on the doorjamb to steady himself.

I assumed that he was lost. Old people got lost all the time. But then he said, "Rosen?" And a younger man came up behind him and confirmed that he had indeed found the Rosen room.

The younger man took Rabbi Taub's arm and led him into the room. My father stepped aside to let them enter. Zippy jumped up, grabbed the chair she'd been sitting in, and motioned toward it.

Rabbi Taub extended a finger, pointing at the side of my bed. Zippy slid the chair over.

The helper man guided the rebbe into the chair.

In what appeared to be slow motion, the ancient rabbi reached out toward me. When he touched my hand, I expected him to disintegrate like an old yellowed piece of paper. But he stayed intact, in the same nominally alive state he'd been in the moment before.

Then we all just sat there, frozen, in an awkward silence. The rebbe looked tired, and I felt like I should offer him the bed, but I wasn't sure I had the strength to get out, and there wasn't really room for both of us.

After a minute, my father came over near the bed, and he reached down to shake Taub's hand. "It's a great honor to have you at my son's bedside," he said. "We deeply appreciate your time and your presence. I'm sure we can agree that although my son's actions have been in violation of Jewish law and of our community's standards, that the trial he has been through has been punishment enough. We certainly understand if the community as a whole is not yet ready to fully accept him. You see, Rebbe, I myself have had trouble understanding his motivations and offering him his own father's forgiveness. However, it should of course be said, that we've made great progress in our project—"

Rabbi Taub cut him off by raising a single finger. "Nu," he said. And then he said a number of other things. They came out in a series of hisses and mutterings, all of them in non-English languages, and I didn't understand a word. He ended it with the same little shift he'd used with me back at the yeshiva: "You see, yes?"

My father at least pretended to see. He nodded, and he moved his eyes. Instead of making direct eye contact with Taub, he moved his eyes down toward the rabbi's feet.

I did not see. I had no idea what the old dude was saying.

Taub went on, talking in a fashion that almost passed as animated. He was even gesticulating, pointing one of his bony fingers at my father. "You see, yes?" he asked again.

My dad nodded again.

But the nod wasn't enough. "Yes?" Taub repeated.

"Yes," my father said. "Yes, Rebbe."

I had no idea what was going on. It was like watching a sport where you don't have any idea what the rules are. You can kind of tell who's winning, but that's about it.

Rabbi Taub kept talking.

I shot Zippy a look. She grabbed her phone and got her thumbs going. Her translations appeared in my phone. Taub says the apartment building is irrelevant in the face of the sickening tragedy, that it's meaningless compared to the lives lost. He says you did the right thing in erasing the cemetery desecrations, and the cherem against you was unjust.

"Yes, yes," my father said.

Dad says yes, Zippy sent, "yes" being a relatively formal affirmative statement.

I speak English, I replied.

Zippy continued: Now Taub says you are a hero for saving human life, no matter who that human is—he cites the Sanhedrin Gemara to emphasize the point.

"Yes, yes," my dad repeated.

Now Rabbi Taub was shaking his extended finger at my father. My dad took a step back as though he'd been pushed. Taub has called Dad a spineless donkey, Zippy explained.

I believe the correct translation is "ass," I corrected her.

Taub's voice suddenly grew scratchy, and it started to fade away. The rabbi's eyes darted around the room, searching. It was my turn to translate. You need to water the rabbi, I sent to Zippy.

She jumped up, hustled out the door, and returned a moment later with a cup. She presented it to Rabbi Taub, who accepted it with a bow of his head. As he drank, water slipped from his mouth, wound down his beard, and dripped onto his chair. We all pretended not to notice.

Taub put the cup down on the table next to the bed and stood up. His helper came over to take the rebbe's arm.

Taub turned to me. "You see, yes?" he asked me.

"Yes, Rebbe," I said, and I watched him leave the room.

My father didn't watch his departure. He was too busy staring at a spot on the wall.

We didn't talk about it. My father led Leah out as soon as the coast was clear. But the next day, when my father tossed me the newspaper, he'd circled two articles. One of them called me a "textbook heretic," but the other one was by a prominent Lakewood rabbi, and it was titled "The Five Important Lessons We Can All Learn From Yehuda Rosen." The rabbi said that my actions displayed important leadership, and could be used as an example of how to carry old traditions into our increasingly modern world.

I skimmed the article while my father stood over the bed. "This is what I've been trying to tell you," I said when I'd finished. "Not that I 'display important leadership' necessarily, just that . . . Just that I was right from the beginning."

My father was silent. He crossed his arms.

"I guess I don't need you to say anything. I just need you to know how I feel, and that I haven't changed my mind."

He was quiet for another moment. "Yehuda, for better or for worse, it's always clear exactly how you feel."

On my last day in the hospital, Anna-Marie came to visit.

After I'd gotten my phone back, we'd sent each other a couple panicked, awkward texts, in which I'd told her I was "ok" and she'd told me she was "ok." But I hadn't seen her until now.

My family was sitting around playing Settlers of Catan. I had just obtained "longest road," so Chana had begun cheating, picking up more resource cards than she was allowed, announcing new and various rules that conveniently favored her. Rivkie didn't understand the game, but she liked to play house with the tiny pieces. She was sitting on Goldie's lap, but Goldie's not much bigger than Rivkie, so it was just one small person sitting on top of another small person. My parents were seated at the little round table in the corner, conferring about something.

Anna-Marie appeared in the doorway. Her mother lurked behind her. Anna-Marie knocked quietly on the doorframe. I looked up from the game. She was wearing long pants, so I couldn't see what kind of shape her legs were in. But she was walking normally, so the gashes must have been healing okay.

My dad looked up at the knock and rose from the chair. When he saw who it was, he almost growled. He looked right past Anna-Marie at her mother. He did his chest puff. He walked to the door with a wide stance like a bodyguard or a bouncer. "How *dare* you come— "

"Avraham," my mother said.

"Dad," said Zippy.

Mrs. Diaz-O'Leary took a step back. "I didn't mean to cause any undue stress. I'll go wait outside. Please let—"

Anna-Marie looked at me, then at the floor, then back at me. "It's okay, Ma. We can go."

"No," I said. "Don't go. You can definitely come in."

Anna-Marie looked relieved and let herself smile awkwardly. She stepped into the room. "I brought kosher Starburst. I see you have plenty of food, but—"

"Starburst aren't food," I said. "I've read the ingredients. It's just sugar and like thirty different chemicals."

"So it's the chemicals that make them so good."

I wanted to introduce Anna-Marie to my family, but my dad wouldn't shake her hand, and the little girls wouldn't know what to make of her, so I didn't. The older people knew who she was.

Zippy gave up her chair to Anna-Marie and took over my place in the game. I would have liked some privacy, but privacy isn't something you get in my kind of family.

We sat in silence for a minute. Neither of us knew what to say. Should we talk about the fight we had? Should we talk about the trauma we went through? Should we talk about our trauma-induced fifteen minutes of fame? Neither of us wanted to talk about any of that. There would be a time for all of those conversations, but this wasn't it.

In a way, it was like the day we'd first met, when neither of us knew what to say. We'd been through a lot together, but after a trauma like that, the kind of trauma that changes you, it almost felt like we were two new people who had to introduce ourselves all over again.

The moment was tense and uncomfortable. I almost wished I hadn't invited her in. But then she blinked her eyes a bunch and said, "Hoodie." Her voice was quiet, almost a whisper.

"Anna-Marie," I whispered back.

"Most of my friends call me Hyphens."

We smiled at each other and the tension evaporated.

"Are *all* of these your sisters?" she asked, eyeing the crowd around the board game.

"Yeah."

"I've always wanted a sister," she said wistfully.

"I can spare one. Let me know if you see one you like."

Anna-Marie giggled.

"May I suggest Chana?" I said.

Chana looked up from the board, a snarl on her lips. "She's an acquired taste," I explained, "for the refined palate. She's the connoisseur's sibling. And she doubles as an effective guard dog."

"I could use one of those. Borneo loves intruders. He loves everybody."

The board game was coming into the homestretch. The older kids were concentrating on the game, so nobody was listening to Rivkie babble. She stole one of Leah's "cities" off the board and brought it over to us, so she could tell us about it.

I acted like I was impressed by the small wooden block she shoved in my face. I asked her how many houses were in the city.

"One," she told me.

"That's a small city," Anna-Marie said.

Rivkie glanced up at Anna-Marie, seeing her for the first time. "The Horowitz family lives there," Rivkie told her. "They have an abba, an eema, ten kids, and twenty cats."

"That must be a foul-smelling household," I said. "I shudder to picture that litter box."

"The cats don't poop," Rivkie explained.

"They must be very constipated," I noted. "I saw an infomercial that said that if you don't poop for two weeks, you start barfing feces. I'm concerned for those felines."

Rivkie nodded solemnly, considering. She hadn't yet learned not to conflate her two eldest siblings. The others knew by now that the stuff I said was mostly bullshit, a cheap attempt to match Zippy's authentic wisdom.

I scooped Rivkie up onto the bed. I ruffled her curls and told her she was my cat, and if she ever suffered extreme constipation of any dangerous duration, I would make sure to buy her laxatives. She had no idea what I was saying, but she thanked me.

I was glad there wasn't a nurse in the room just then, because the nurses had told me, in no uncertain terms, that I was not permitted to "manhandle" any of my visitors.

"Can you catch?" I asked Anna-Marie, winding up to throw my sister to her. My shoulder burned in pain, but I was committed.

Anna-Marie flinched. "Yeah, but I don't catch . . . people."

"If you want a sister, you'll have to learn."

Anna-Marie laughed. "Okay. But let's not practice in front of your family. I think they hate me enough already. I don't want to drop your sister."

"That's fair," I told her. So I spilled Rivkie off the bed onto the floor.

Anna-Marie gasped and reached for Rivkie, but Rivkie had already popped up, and was climbing up the side of the bed so she could be tossed off again.

Anna-Marie was aghast. She looked around the room like she'd found herself in some kind of zoo exhibit, suddenly surrounded by strange creatures. But she wasn't looking at the door. She wasn't trying to get away.

There were many weird things about being in the hospital. For example, my room at home didn't have *any* bad paintings of barns. But my hospital room had three. Another thing was that, for the first time in my life, there wasn't anybody around forcing me to pray. Nobody asked me if I said the Shema at night. Nobody checked in the morning to see if I prayed Shacharis.

Zippy brought me a prayer book and my tefillin, but the doctor said I wasn't allowed to use the tefillin.

So for the first time in my life, prayer was my choice. And I wasn't planning to do it. I hadn't prayed when I was barely conscious in the ICU, and nothing horrible had happened to me. I thought maybe I'd skip it, even if it was just for the novelty. Sometimes you do stuff—or don't do stuff—just because you can.

For example, the second morning in recovery, I skipped the morning service. I left my prayer book on the table next to the bed. But then as I shifted around in the bed, trying to find the least painful position, I started reliving the shooting, as I do just about every day, as I'll probably do for years.

That's the worst part of the trauma for me, the constant reliving, the instant replay, looping endlessly. The trauma counselor says that's really common. And I'm lucky: when I replay the attack, I don't have regrets. Lots of people wish they could have acted differently, found a way to save people or stop the violence. But I get a little bit of comfort because I know I did the right thing. I did what I could, helping Anna-Marie, but there wasn't anything I could have done for Elad or Mr. Abramowitz or Mrs. Goldberg. I think about them all the time. I carry their memories with me everywhere I go. But I know I couldn't have saved them.

On that morning, the scene I kept seeing over and over was the part where Mr. Abramowitz, with his hands up in the air, took a bullet in his neck. Over and over in my mind I watched him raise his hands, and saw the hole appear in his neck, just below his jaw. The neck is *so* exposed. It's a serious design flaw.

I got lost reliving Mr. Abramowitz's death, and before I knew it, I was saying the Kaddish. The Kaddish is the prayer of mourning. Unlike most prayers, you speak the Kaddish to other people, not to God. It's a call and response with the whole congregation.

You aren't allowed to pray the Kaddish alone. You need a congregation. You need a minyan.

I thought about Zippy, a young woman, praying with tefillin, violating and fulfilling a commandment at the same time. I guess that's what I was doing, praying the Kaddish alone in my hospital room. But I didn't feel the violation part. It felt right—it felt fulfilling—to mourn loss in my own way. Meaning didn't have to come from someone else's religious teachings. It was something I could find in myself.

CHAPTER 15

in which I sit on the side in a lawn chair,
both literally and figuratively

ZIPPY AND YOEL GOT MARRIED a month later. I invited Anna-Marie to the wedding. Actually, I'm not sure that's true. I think she just invited herself. The wedding was on the lawn at the yeshiva and Hyphens was all, Hey, I live right there. Maybe I'll just walk by in a cute dress and somebody will invite me in.

Since the hospital visit, things between us weren't too awkward, and she and I texted sometimes. I highly doubt it. Also, your "cute" dress better go down past your knees, have long sleeves past the elbows, and have a high neckline. Does it meet that description?

No, she sent. I guess I'll have to get another one.

No, you won't. Because you're not invited.

Now that I'm thinking about it, it was Zippy who invited her, or insisted that I invite her.

At first I was offended by Anna-Marie's fascination with my family, with my religion. It made me feel less like a real person. It felt like Anna-Marie was looking at me in one of those dioramas at a museum. I also suspected that part of the reason she liked spending time with me was that it made her mother so upset.

But then, didn't I also find her interesting for more or less the same reasons? And even though my other friends were allowed to talk to me again, it was tough to communicate with them when I never saw them.

I was out of school for the rest of the marking period, because I had physical therapy and trauma counseling almost every day. I was supposed to be doing my schoolwork "asynchronously," which I think means "not at all."

Also, it made my dad furious anytime Anna-Marie was around, but he couldn't do anything about it because of what Rabbi Taub had said. If I had Chana's instincts, I think I would tack up pictures of Anna-Marie all over the house, just to torture him. If I had more money, I could buy a life-size cardboard cutout of her, and station her in the kitchen next to the coffee maker.

Plus, the trauma counselor said it was good for me and Anna-Marie to spend time together. Even if we didn't talk about the trauma itself, being together could help us process it.

The thing about the wedding, though, was that we weren't allowed to be together. Just like in synagogue, the sexes are separate at weddings. I was on the men's side, and under normal circumstances I would have been dancing with Yoel, and my dad, and everybody else. But my left arm was still in a sling, and it hurt to dance.

I sat off to the side, sipping juice from a plastic cup. I was busy thinking about the irony that I was the one who'd saved the apartment project, that when the rest of the community moved in next fall, it would be because of me. Nobody would thank me, but thanks to Rabbi Taub, people would make eye contact with me again, which was pretty cool—it's nice when people acknowledge your existence.

I was lost in thought, so it took me a minute to notice Moshe Tzvi pulling up a chair next to me. He was sweaty from dancing. I'd only seen him a couple times since the . . . event, and only at the synagogue. We hadn't spoken a single time. I was still angry at him for not visiting me in the hospital.

He didn't look at me. I didn't look at him. We both just faced the dance floor, watching everybody with their elbows locked together, spinning around in their suits.

I'd been watching it for almost an hour, the dancing. I'd danced at the Wasserstein wedding the year before, twirling around with friends and family. I'd felt a part of it then, like I fit right in. But now I felt outside of it, and wasn't sure where I fit, if I fit at all.

"Fit" was the right word. The whole thing was like a jacket that didn't fit me right anymore. But it was the only one I had. I was naked underneath it. I didn't really want to wear it, but I couldn't take it off either, because then what would I have?

"Hi," said Moshe Tzvi.

I said nothing. I could tell he was uncomfortable, and I wanted him to stay that way.

"Hoodie," he said. He had to talk pretty loud to be heard over the music.

"Speak, Moshe Tzvi. If you have something to say, say it."

"Fine, fine. Very well. I just want to tell you that I didn't visit you because . . . My father and I have a difference of opinion. I . . . After the whole *thing*, I went back into the Sanhedrin Gemara to understand it better myself. It says that if you save one Jewish soul, you save all of humanity. That told me that the Jewish soul matters above all. And I still believe that. But right after it says that, it says the same thing, but without the Jewish part. It says that if you save a soul, you have saved humanity. There's no modifier. It just says 'soul.' It could be any soul, Jewish or gentile."

We sat in silence for a minute.

"Is that your way of apologizing?" I asked. "Are you telling me you'll stand by me?"

He said nothing. I took that as a yes.

"Very well," I said. "I accept your apology." I didn't see that I really had a choice.

He looked like he was expecting a handshake or a hug. But I left him hanging. I wanted him to stay uncomfortable a little longer.

"I'm glad to hear you're progressing in your studies," I told him. Then I took out my phone to signal that the conversation was over. I acted like I'd just received a text message, squinting at the phone, pretending to read. But then I received a real one. It was Anna-Marie. I think I'm going home, she sent.

Do you want to conveniently pass by my chair on your way out? I sent.

She didn't reply, but I could see her making her way around the side of one of the modular buildings. Moshe Tzvi saw her coming too. I could see the fear in his eyes. He got up, patted me on the shoulder, and walked back to the dance floor.

I pushed Moshe Tzvi's lawn chair a few feet away from mine, so Anna-Marie wouldn't be sitting right next to me. She sat down. A look of relief spread out across her face. "One thing I don't get," she said, "is that married couples are allowed to touch each other, right? But then they can't dance together at a wedding."

"You aren't going to touch each other in public," I told her. "You don't flaunt your bodies."

She looked at me, trying to figure out, as always, if I agreed with that interpretation or not, if it would offend me if she criticized it.

"It just doesn't feel *important* to me," she said. "There are only so many things you can care about. Why spend your time caring about things that seem . . . not important?"

"If you believe that God cares about it, then it's the *most* important thing," I said.

"I guess," she said. "It's not any different from the stuff my mom acts crazy about." She was quiet for a moment. "I don't want to be a fanatic, Hoodie. I want to be reasonable. I want to continue to care about things that matter. Are we all just destined to be fanatics about something?"

"I don't know that 'destined' is the right word. You have *some* say. But that's the part that's hard: the choice. When you're a kid, all of those choices are made *for* you. Somebody else chooses the path. And then once you reach the age where you can unmake those choices, you've already gone pretty far. It's a long road back."

"Don't you think it's worth it, though? So you can be who you are? Or at least who you want to be?"

"Yeah. I agree. But there's still a small part of me that wishes I didn't *have* to make any of those choices. It's like, if I were bit by a rabid raccoon right now, and I started just, like, foaming at the mouth, I wouldn't have to worry about any of it. It would all be out of my hands. And it would be *easier.* I could just start dancing with you, and nobody would care, because it wouldn't be my choice anymore, due to my rabidity."

We sat in silence for a minute. Or, it wasn't silence. The music was pumping. You could probably hear it a mile away.

We weren't supposed to be sitting *with* each other, so we weren't facing exactly the same way. But Anna-Marie sneaked a look at me. "Wait. So, in this scenario, I'm dancing with a *rabid* person? Why exactly am I doing that?"

"Yeah, I hear you. That seems like an unwise choice on your part." I laughed. "My point was only that . . . You know what? Forget it. Should we see if I can smuggle us some wine?"

"Yes, please," said Anna-Marie. "I thought coming to the wedding would make Monica angry enough. But if I come home drunk, that'll . . . Man. That'll be *fire*."

I walked over to the drinks table, took two plastic cups, and filled them with kosher wine. It wasn't really smuggling. At a wedding, if you were tall enough to reach the wine table, you were allowed to drink the wine. I didn't actually like wine, but Anna-Marie seemed excited about it.

Back at the lawn chairs, I handed a cup to Anna-Marie. She took a tentative sip and grimaced. "That is *way* too sweet."

"Look, if you have a better way to dye your teeth purple, I'm open to suggestions."

Anna-Marie smiled at me over the brim of her cup. "Walk me home?"

I took a glance back at the celebration. Everybody was dancing. Nobody was looking at us. Nobody would miss me. I nodded and we started the short stroll.

Hyphens led me down the lawn and onto the street, but where we would have turned left to walk the half block to her house, she went straight instead. We walked up the street, past *our* tree, though I doubted that she thought of the tree that way.

We walked in silence. The only sounds were the clop of our dress shoes on the sidewalk and the distant hum of the music.

It's funny: Getting shot compares favorably to getting rejected by the girl you love. When Anna-Marie told me that she didn't like me back, that she never had, I thought I never wanted to see her again, that I could never feel comfortable around her.

But strolling through the neighborhood with her, I felt just like I did when I was hanging out on her couch a while back. I felt at home. Outside of Zippy, Anna-Marie was the only person I'd fully opened up to. And she was the only person who shared my trauma, who'd been with me through the horror, through the worst moment of my life. There was something comforting about being with somebody you didn't have to hide anything from.

The walk only got awkward when we reached her house. Anna-Marie stood at the curb, looking up into my eyes. When we'd first met we were exactly the same height, but I'd grown a half inch in the last month or two.

She took a gulp from her cup, then flashed me a purple smile. "Can you smell the wine on my breath?" she asked, and she leaned in closer.

I could. She smelled sweet, from the wine and from some other more human scent. It was intoxicating, and not just because wine was literally intoxicating. "No," I lied.

"Crap. I want to make sure my mom notices." The sun was going down, and the house behind her was dark and lifeless. Anna-Marie took another sip. Then she leaned in closer, bringing her lips closer to me. "How about now?" she asked.

And then her lips were on mine, and my hand was on her hip, and her hand was on my arm, which was extraordinarily painful. But at least the wine tasted better this way.

As we wrapped our arms around each other, and pressed our mouths together, I tallied up the halachic violations, but it was hard to count with her fingers on the nape of my neck.

In the ambulance, I'd told God that I wouldn't break any of his commandments ever again. I didn't even try to justify the violation of my promise. I just hoped God was otherwise occupied and didn't happen to see the two kids kissing on the curb of the quiet suburban street.

After a moment, we both pulled back and stood at arm's length. My heart was pounding and my breath came quick and short. Over Anna-Marie's shoulder, I saw a light flick on in the house. It revealed the mayor, standing at the living room window, glaring.

Anna-Marie looked back, saw her mom, and grinned at her. Then she took a step back toward me, putting her arm on mine, coming in for another go.

I winced and pulled back. "I'm sorry, it's just my arm. If you'll recall, I received a bullet wound therein, and it hurts when you—"

"Oh, sorry, I . . ."

But the arm thing was a lie. That wasn't why I was pulling back. Kissing Anna-Marie was absolutely spectacular, and if I was going to keep doing it, I'd happily tolerate the extreme clavicular discomfort.

I just wasn't sure I was ready for what kissing her would mean. I wasn't sure I was ready to give up the best friend I'd just gotten back, the community that was mostly accepting me again, the family that was welcoming me back into the fold. They could handle me hanging out with her, but *this* was a whole different thing. Also, there was probably a limit to the number of commandments I was willing to break at any one time.

Plus, if I ever kissed Anna-Marie again, I wanted it to be because we loved each other. And when Hyphens turned around to make sure her mom was watching, it made me wonder how much of the kiss was pro-me, and how much was anti-Monica.

"That's not true, actually," I said. "I mean, it *does* hurt. But that's not why I—I just . . . I just don't know if I can go there yet. I guess I don't know for certain if I ever will. I'm just not sure, and I don't think it would be fair to you to leave you in a situation where I'm waffling back and forth. It's that choice thing I was talking about with the raccoon. Or, it's like a jacket, but you're naked underneath it, so even if you don't *like* the jacket, taking it off is kind of a big—"

"Hoodie?"

"And remember when you were telling me that you could be honest with me *because* we're from different places? When I thought about it later, it hurt, because I thought it wasn't about *me*. It was just about who I was. But now I get it, and I feel that way too. We have something that's ours, and belongs to nobody else, and I just don't want to—"

"Hoodie."

"Yeah?"

"You can stop. I get it."

She patted me on the other shoulder, took a final gulp from her cup, and turned up the front walk where the lawn sign used to be.

I watched her from the curb while her mom watched her from the window. When the mayor turned her eyes to me, I waved to her. She stepped back from the window and went to open the door for her daughter.

I started up the street, feeling empty. I headed toward the wedding where there was enough food to fill me.

After the wedding, Zippy moved out. I'd always thought that when she left, the house would grow dark and cold in her absence. And it did grow dark and cold for me, but not just because she was gone. When she left, she took her laptop and my father disconnected the Wi-Fi, and I was plunged back into the dark ages.

I lost my main connection to the world. With the Wi-Fi, I'd gotten used to seeing the news, scrolling through commentary, reading the antisemitic vitriol of internet trolls. It was disturbing, but at least I knew what was going on.

There were other issues too. Suddenly, I was the oldest. Being the oldest kid in the family carried many important responsibilities. For example, sometimes my mom would text me from upstairs, telling me to "preheat the oven to 350." And I'd have to figure out (without the aid of Rabbi Google) which one was the oven, and how to turn it on, and, like, 350 *what?*

"Degrees," apparently. That's what Zippy told me over the phone. I usually just called Zippy. "Fahrenheit" she clarified. "Actually," she went on, "today is a good day for you to mess up. I would like you to burn the garlic bread."

"You *want* me to burn—"

"Yes, beyond recognition. So it fills the whole house with the smell of burning. I need an excuse to come over and save the day. I have something for you."

I did as I was told. I totally "forgot" to set a timer and only "remembered" when I saw the smoke coming out of the oven in little tendrils.

It was hard to pretend to forget something like that. I wasn't going back to school until the second marking period, and I was pretty bored. I'd resorted to reading Jewish books, which, in my defense, were the only reading material in the house unless you counted, like, the back of the shampoo bottles, or my schoolwork.

When my mom came to the top of the stairs to inform me that the burning smell was "distracting" her from her work, I assured her that Zippy would be over any minute to fix the problem.

Zippy made an excellent dinner: pasta, garlic bread, salad. Afterward, she and I cleaned up the kitchen while my parents retreated upstairs to work, and the girls went outside to see what sort of grass-stain or mud challenges they could provide for the family's new launderer (me).

When the dishes were on the drying rack, and the sun was down, and the kitchen was dark, Zippy and I were alone at the table. We sat in silence for a moment. Then Zippy reached down into her bag at the base of her chair. She removed a rect-angular object, placed it on the table, and slid it over to me.

It took a second for my eyes to adjust in the dark, before I could see it right. It was an iPhone. "What's this?" I asked.

"It's a smartphone, Hoodie. Surely you've *seen* them at some—"

"No, I know what it *is*. I just . . ." A couple of my friends had smartphones, but theirs all had filters on them that basically made them flip phones without the hinge.

"I have to get back, and I have no idea when Dad will come downstairs. So I'll make this brief. The phone is unfiltered. And for your purposes it's untraceable, since it's on Yoel's and my plan. This is the *pure* stuff, Hoodie. If you—I don't know—if you want porn, it'll show you porn."

"Can you be more specific in those directions?" I asked. "Just, you know, for curiosity's sake, how does one find the porn? Can I just ask Siri? Siri, show me porn."

I was joking, but Zippy didn't laugh. "You have to turn it on first," she said.

"I think that was just my weird way of saying thank you."

"I know," she said. She looked out of the kitchen into the dark hallway. She spoke quickly and quietly. "Listen, it's not perfect, this religion, this life. If you expect the tradition to be perfect, it will disappoint you. If you expect the people around you to be pure and pious, they'll disappoint you too. But there isn't one way to do this. Don't listen to anybody who tells you otherwise. And there are ways around things. There are VPNs that get around Wi-Fi filters. There are secret unfiltered phones. What you do with those things is up to you. You can watch porn with Siri, or you can stream Talmud lessons on YouTube. That's your choice. Anyway, that's all I've got."

I booted up the phone.

Zippy got up, slung her bag over her shoulder, and walked

toward the kitchen door, where she stopped. "One more thing," she said. "Just so we're clear, if Dad finds out about this, I will deny it."

"You'll just lie about the phone?" I asked.

"What phone? I don't know what you're talking about. No good could possibly come of a thing like that. The only way to a righteous life is through strict obedience and self-denial of temptation."

Zippy disappeared out of the house. I disappeared upstairs to my bedroom.

I spent the next hour downloading and scrolling through different social media apps. Then, before I could chicken out, I took a picture of myself lying in my bed and sent it to Anna-Marie. Look, I'm posting my first selfie. Am I doing it right?

I hadn't talked to Anna-Marie since our aborted wine kiss, and I was worried that she wouldn't respond. Other than the phone, she was my only connection to that other world. And she was the only person who'd gone through my trauma with me. And I liked her. She was important to me. I needed her to reply.

A few minutes went by. But just as I was convincing myself that I'd never hear from her again, she texted back.

Lmfao, she sent back, along with a bunch of laugh-crying emojis. You didn't "post" anything. You just sent me a creepy picture of yourself from a number I don't even know, which is low-key stalker behavior. And tbh, the little mustache ur growing only makes it worse.

I beamed at the phone.

Then I sent her a looping video/image thing of a baby dancing on a table, and then one of a cat knocking something off a table, then a dog typing on a laptop, then a woman at an office desk celebrating with her arms in the air. How about now? I texted. Am I doing it right now?

She sent me a loop of a woman shaking her head furiously. I think you're coachable. We can start by working on your gif game. The key is just not to use them. Ever.

I put the phone down next to me and stared up at the ceiling. I took a moment to get lost in the plaster's water stains and winding cracks.

I wondered if I still loved her. I wasn't sure. Maybe she was right when she told me I had no idea what love actually was—Anna-Marie was right a lot. All I knew was that I needed her in my life, and maybe that need was a love of sorts.

The phone buzzed on the bedspread. It was another message from Anna-Marie, a link of some sort.

I clicked it. It was a web page, part of the NYU website. When I scrolled down I saw why she'd sent it. There was a section on "Dual Degree Partnerships." It said that NYU had an agreement with Yeshiva University where NYU students could take classes at YU, and vice versa.

We can take classes together? I sent.

Yeah, she replied. But you'll have to come down to NYU. I don't own any long skirts.

I'd have to work on my grades to get into YU, but I didn't tell that to Hyphens. College was still a couple years down the

215

road. What mattered was that I'd get to be friends with her until then.

I sent her a picture of two Spider-Men pointing at each other. Have you seen this meme?

Obvs. I've seen all the memes, Hoodie.

Can you explain it to me?

How much time do you have?

All the time, hyphens, all the time. If I had my choice, I'd just text nonstop with Anna-Marie until the sunset on Friday. And then, well, I guess I'd cross that bridge—or not cross it— when I got there.

ACKNOWLEDGMENTS

A book is a team effort, and this novel wouldn't exist without the incredible work of some truly special people. My deepest, sincerest thanks to . . .

My agent, Rena Rossner. I knew from the moment we first spoke that you were the perfect champion for this project, and for me. Thank you for helping me revise my manuscript and for finding such a wonderful place for it, all while dealing with my substantial neuroses. I'm so happy to have you in my corner.

My editor, Talia Benamy. You brought this story to life with your editorial vision. I'm consistently impressed and, frankly, shamed by your dedication, generosity, and attention to detail. Thank you for guiding this book into the world. I'm so grateful.

The brilliant folks at Philomel and Penguin Random House. The design team: Lily Qian, Anna Booth, Monique Sterling, and Ellice Lee, for making this book look so cool. The copyeditors: Abigail Powers, Marinda Valenti, and Sola Akinlana, for making this book make sense. Gaby Corzo for keeping it all connected, Lathea Mondesir for getting the word out, and Jill Santopolo and Ken Wright for making the whole thing possible.

Roz Warren. Thank you for reading every word I've ever written, and for encouraging me to delete most of them. You've improved each of my manuscripts with your honesty, your sense of humor, and your sharp eye. To be clear, the sharp eye I'm talking about is figurative. Your literal vision is alarmingly poor. I worry about it.

Michael Deagler and Rob Volansky. Without you I might have quit writing years ago. The writing life can be lonely and discouraging, and I'd be wandering alone in the dark without the camaraderie and support your friendship provides. And that's to say nothing of the significant ways you've helped me grow as a writer over the last decade. I owe you both so much.

Lauren Grodstein and the Rutgers-Camden MFA program, and not just for introducing me to Mike and Rob. Lauren, you told me that if writing was important to me, I needed to make it a priority. That was sage advice at a pivotal point, when I needed to decide how I would go about structuring my early adult life. Your mentorship in those days was vital to me, and I'm so appreciative.

My family: my wife, parents, sister, grandparents. You've supported me in more ways than I can count, and I'll never be able to thank you enough.

You, the person who just read this book, for helping make my lifelong dream come true. I hope you enjoyed it. And if you didn't, I apologize. Customer satisfaction is important to me. I'll try to do better next time.